LITTLE CITIZENS

The Humours of School Life

MYRA KELLY

1st WORLD
LIBRARY
Literary Society

Little Citizens

Myra Kelly

© 1st World Library – Literary Society, 2004
PO Box 2211
Fairfield, IA 52556
www.1stworldlibrary.org
First Edition

LCCN: 2004091264

Softcover ISBN: 1-59540-682-4
eBook ISBN: 1-59540-782-0

Purchase *"Little Citizens"*
as a traditional bound book at:
www.1stWorldLibrary.org/purchase.asp?ISBN=1-59540-682-4

1st World Library Literary Society is a nonprofit organization dedicated to promoting literacy by:

- Creating a free internet library accessible from any computer worldwide.
- Hosting writing competitions and offering book publishing scholarships.

Readers interested in supporting literacy through sponsorship, donations or membership please contact:
literacy@1stworldlibrary.org
Check us out at: www.1stworldlibrary.org

TO MY MOTHER

CONTENTS

A Little Matter of Real Estate 7

The Uses of Adversity 23

A Christmas Present for a Lady 37

Love Among the Blackboards 48

Morris and the Honourable Tim 67

When a Man's Widowed 86

H.R.H. The Prince of Hester Street 104

The Land Of Heart's Desire 127

A Passport to Paradise 148

The Touch of Nature. 167

A LITTLE MATTER OF REAL ESTATE

Four weeks of teaching in a lower East Side school had deprived Constance Bailey of many of the "Ideals in Education" which, during four years at college, she had trustingly acquired. But, despite many discourage-ments, despite an unintelligible dialect and an autocratic "Course of Study," she clung to an ambition to establish harmony in her kingdom and to impress a high moral tone upon the fifty-eight little children of Israel entrusted to her care. She was therefore troubled and heavy of heart when it was borne in upon her that two of her little flock - cousins to boot, and girls - had so far forgotten the Golden Rule as to be "mad on theirselves und wouldn't to talk even," as that Bureau of Fashionable Intelligence, Sarah Schrodsky, duly reported.

"Und Teacher," Sarah continued, "Eva Gonorowsky's mamma has a mad on Sadie Gonorowsky's mamma, und her papa has a mad on her papa, und her gran'ma has a mad on both of papas und both of mammas, und her gran'pa has a mad somethin' fierce on both of uncles, und her auntie - "

Here Miss Bailey sent the too communicative Sarah to her place and called the divided house of Gonorowsky to her desk for instant judgment. And as she held forth she was delighted to see that her words were falling upon good ground, for the dark and dainty features of her hearers expressed a flattering degree of conviction and of humility. She was admiring the wonderful lashes lying damp and dark on Eva's smooth cheek when the beautiful eyes unclosed, gazed straight across the desk at Sadie, and Eva took a flying leap into Teacher's lap to cling with arms and knees and fingers to her chosen refuge.

"Oh, Teacher, Teacher," she wailed, "Sadie makes on me such a snoot I got a scare over it."

Miss Bailey turned to the so lately placid face of Sadie in search of the devastating "snoot," but met only a serene glance of conscious guilelessness and the assurance:

"No ma'an, I don't makes no snoot on nobody. I get killed as anything off of my mamma sooner I makes a snoot. It ain't polite." This with a reassuring smile and direct and candid gaze.

"Teacher, yiss ma'an, she makes all times a snoot on me," cried the now weeping Eva, "all times. She turns her nose around, und makes go away her eyes, und comes her tongue out long. On'y I dassent to fight mit her while I'm cousins mit her. Und over cousins you got all times kind feelings."

"Well, Sadie," Teacher questioned, "what have you to say?"

The dark eyes met Teacher's with no shadow in their depths as Sadie uttered her denial:

"I *never* in my world done no snoot."

A shudder of admiring awe swept over the assembled class - followed by a gasp of open contradiction as Sadie went on with her vindication. For Sadie's snoots were the envy of all the class. Had not Morris Mogilewsky paid three cents for lessons in the art, and, with the accomplishment, frightened a baby into what its angry mother described as "spine-yell convulsions"? And now Sadie was saying, "I *couldn't* to make no snoot. Never. But, Teacher, it's like this: Eva makes *me* whole bunches of trouble. Bertha Binderwitz und me is monitors in the yard when the childrens comes back from dinner. So-o-oh, I says, 'front dress,' like you says, so the childrens shall look on what head is in front of them. On'y Eva she don't 'front dress' at all, but extra she longs out her neck und rubs on me somethin' fierce - "

"It's a lie!" interrupted Eva gently. "I don't make nothing like that. I stands by my line und Sadie she makes faces on me with her hand. It ain't polite." This with plaintive self-righteousness. "No ma'an, it *ain't* polite - you makes snoots mit your hand like this." And as Eva illustrated with outspread fingers and a pink thumb in juxtaposition to a diminutive nose, Teacher, with uncertain gravity, was forced to admit that snoots of that description are sanctioned by few books of etiquette.

"Now, my dear little girls," said she, "this quarrelling must stop. I want you to kiss each other as cousins should."

This suggestion was a distinct failure. Eva and Sadie, with much fluttering of aprons and waving of curls, sought opposite corners of the schoolroom, while up started Sarah Schrodsky with: "Teacher, they couldn't to make no kissing. They're mad on theirselves 'cause their mammas has a mad. Sadie's mamma says like this on Eva's mamma, 'Don't you dast to talk to me - you lives by the fifth floor und your man is a robber.' Und Eva's mamma says - "

When Teacher had managed to silence Sarah she led the weeping Gonorowskys back to their places and the scholastic world wagged on in outward tranquillity.

Hostilities were temporarily suspended some days later owing to the illness of Sadie, by far the more aggressive of the opposing parties. Eva led a placid life for three peaceful days, and then - as by law prescribed and postal card invited - Sadie's mother came to explain her daughter's absence. Large of person, bland of manner, in a heavy black shawl and a heavier black wig, Mrs. Lazarus Gonorowsky stood beaming and bobbing in the hall.

"I likes I should Sadie Gonorowsky's teacher see," she began, in the peculiar English of the adult population of the East Side. Mrs. Gonorowsky could neither use nor understand her young daughter's copious invective. Upon being assured that the diminutive form before her was indeed clothed with authority, she announced:

"Comes a letter I should by the school come. I was Sadie's mamma." Here she drew from the inner recesses of the black shawl a bundle which, being placed in a perpendicular position, proved to be the most recent addition to the Gonorowsky household. She smoothed it with a work-worn but tender hand, and repeated in a saddened voice: "Yes, ma'am, I was her mamma und she lays now on the bed."

The increasing sadness of Mrs. Gonorowsky's announcement and its sinister phraseology startled Teacher. "Not dead!" she cried. "Oh, surely not dead!"

"Sure not," was the indignant response. "She's got such a sickness she must lay on the bed, und comes the doctor. Sadie's papa holds much on that child, Miss Teacher, und all times he has a worry over her. Me too. She comes by the school tomorrow maybe, und I ask you by a favour you should do me the kindness to look on her. So she feel again sick she should better on the house come. She say, 'Oh, mamma, I got a lovely teacher; I likes to look on her the while she has such a light face.'"

Having thus diplomatically led up to a question, Mrs. Gonorowsky with great suavity asked, "Sadie is a good girl, hein?"

"Oh, yes, indeed."

"She is shmardt, hein? She don't make you no troubles?"

"Well," Miss Bailey answered, "she has rather bothered me lately by quarrelling with her little cousin, Eva."

"So-o-oh!" exclaimed Sadie's parent ponderously. "So-o-oh, Eva Gonorowsky makes you troubles; she is a bad girl - I tell Sadie - Sadie is a good girl - I tell her she should make nothings with Eva soch a bad girl. For what you not put her back by baby class? She is not shmardt."

"Oh, but she is; she is a bright little thing," cried

Teacher. "I couldn't think of putting her back. She's a dear little girl and I can't imagine why Sadie quarrels with her."

Mrs. Gonorowsky drew her ample form to a wonderful erectness, readjusted her shawl, and answered with much stateliness:

"It was a trouble from off of real estate." With dignity and blandness she proceeded to kiss Teacher's hand, and signified entire willingness to entrust her precious Sadie to the care of so estimable a young person, inquired solicitously if the work were not too much for so small a lady, and cautioned the young person against rainy mornings. Had she a mackintosh? Mr. Gonorowsky was selling them off that week. Were her imperceptibles sufficiently warm? Mr. Gonorowsky, by a strange chance, was absolutely giving away "fine all from wool" imperceptibles, and the store was near. Mrs. Gonorowsky then withdrew, leaving a kindly sentiment in Teacher's heart and an atmosphere of ironing-boards and onions in the hall. On the following morning Sadie returned to her "light-faced" teacher, and for one whole day hostilities were suspended.

But on the morning after this truce Eva was absent from her accustomed place and Sadie blandly disclaimed all knowledge of her whereabouts. After the noon recess a pathetic little figure wavered in the doorway with one arm in a sling and one eye in a poultice. The remaining eye was fixed in deep reproach on the face of Isidore Belchatosky, the Adonis of the class, and the eye was the eye of Eva.

"Eva!" exclaimed Teacher, "oh, Eva, what can you have been doing? What's the matter with your eye?"

"Isidore Belchatosky he goes und makes me this here shiner," said Eva's accusing voice, as the eye under the poultice was uncovered for a moment. It was indeed a "shiner" of aggravated aspect, and Isidore cringed as it met his affrighted gaze. The sling and the bandages were of gay chintz, showing forth the adventures of Robinson Crusoe, and their lurid colours made them horribly conspicuous. Friday scampered across Eva's forehead, pursued by savages; and Crusoe, under his enormous umbrella, nestled close to her heart.

"Surely Isidore would never hit a little girl?" Teacher remonstrated.

"Teacher, yiss ma'an; he makes me this here shiner. Sadie she goes und tells him she kisses him a kiss so he makes me a shiner. He's lovin' mit her und she's got kind feelin's by him, the while his papa's got a candy cart. It's a stylish candy cart mit a bell und a horn. So-o-oh I was yesterday on the store for buy my mamma some wurst, und I don't make nothings mit nobody."

Here the poor, half-blind Eva, with her love and talent for pantomime, took a gay little walk past Teacher's desk, with tossing head and swinging skirts. Then with a cry she recoiled from the very memory of her wrongs.

"Come Isidore! Und he hits me a hack on my leg so I couldn't to hold it even. So I falls und I make me this here shiner. Und when my mamma seen how comes such a bile on my bone she had a mad; she hollered somethin' fierce."

One could well sympathize with the harassed Mrs. Nathan Gonorowsky.

"So-o-oh," continued Eva with melancholy enjoyment, "my mamma she puts medsin at a rag und bangages up mine eye. Und now I ain't healthy."

"Sadie Gonorowsky, come here!" commanded Miss Bailey, in a voice which lifted Sadie bodily from the place to which she had guiltily determined to cling. And Sadie went, jaunty of air, but with shifting eyes.

"Isidore Belchatosky, come here!" commanded Miss Bailey, and Isidore slunk after his divinity.

Teacher was savagely angry, but bylaws forbade corporal punishment, and principles - and the Principal - forbade noisy upbraidings. And so with long, strange words, to supply the element of dread uncertainty, she began to speak, slowly and coldly as one ever should when addressing ears accustomed to much sputtering profanity.

"Sadie and Isidore, did you dare to interfere with the life, the liberty and the happiness of our cherished young friend, Eva Gonorowsky? Did you *dare*?"

"No ma'an," said Sadie with a sob.

"It's a lie!" said Isidore with a snuffle.

"Did you, Isidore, allow yourself to be tempted by beauty to such inconceivable depravity as to blacken Eva's eye?"

"No ma'an. Self done it."

"Did you, Sadie, descend so low as to barter kisses with Isidore Belchatosky?"

"No ma'an," this with much scorn. "I wouldn't to kiss him; he's a scare-cat, und he tells out."

"What did he tell?" asked Teacher.

"He tells out how I say I kiss him a kiss so he make Eva a shiner. Und I wouldn't to do it. Never. So he gave me five cents even, I wouldn't to kiss no scare-cat."

"Well, then, why did you promise?"

"'Cause I couldn't to hit her mineself," said the doughty Sadie. She was inches taller than her victim, and stout withal. "I couldn't, 'cause I ain't so healthy; I'm a nervous child, Teacher, und I was day-before-yesterday sick on the bed."

Here the plaintive plaintiff showed a desire to testify once more, and Teacher appointed three-thirty that afternoon as the hour most suitable for a thorough examination of the case.

When the last arm had been twisted into the last sleeve, when the last chin had been tied into the last shawl, when the last dispute as to ownership in disreputable mittens had been settled, the great case of Gonorowsky vs. Gonorowsky was called. On either side of the desk stood a diminutive Gonorowsky; Eva still plaintive, and Sadie, redly, on the defensive. Directly in front stood that labourer defrauded of his hire, that tool in the hands of guileful woman - Isidore Belchatosky.

"Now," Teacher began, "I want to hear nothing but the truth. Isidore, did you hit Eva?"

"Yiss ma'an."

"What for?"

"For a kiss."

"From whom?"

Here Sadie muttered a threat "to lay him down dead if he tells," and Isidore required promise of safe conduct to his own block before he consented to murmur:

"Sadie Gonorowsky."

"Did you get the kiss?"

"No ma'an."

"Do you know anything about this fight?"

"No ma'an."

"Well, then, you may go home now, and bring your mother with you to-morrow morning."

Isidore left with a heavy heart and the enquiry was continued.

"What has Sadie been doing to you, Eva?" asked Teacher, and Eva, with resigned mien, answered:

"All things," and then details followed. "She makes on me a snoot, she pulls me on the bottom of my hair, she goes und takes her pencil und gives me a stick in my face. When I was marchin' she extra takes her shoes und steps at my legs; I got two swollen legs over her.

Und now" - here a sob - "you could to look on how she makes me biles und shiners."

As Eva's voice droned out these many accusations, Sadie grew more emphatic in her favourite repartee:

"It's a lie! It's a lie! It's a lie!"

"And now, Eva, will you tell me *why* Sadie has been doing all these naughty things?"

"Teacher, I don't know."

"Oh, yes; you do!"

"No ma'an; I don't. I could swear if I do. I kiss up to God." She wafted a kiss towards the ceiling. "I got all times a kind feelin' over Sadie, on'y she wouldn't to be glad on me. I seen yesterday her little brother in the street mit Sadie und she make he shouldn't to talk to me. My heart it breaks when she make like that; I'm got no brother und no sister und I'm lovin' *so* much mit my little cousin. She goes und makes he should say nothin' und in *mine* eyes stands tears. I was sad."

"Well, dear, that's a shame," said Teacher, "and if you really don't understand, go out into the assembly room and wait for me. Sadie is going to tell me all about it."

Eva vanished, only to return with the lurid bandage in her hand and the query: - "Can I make this wet?"

Upon receiving permission so to do she retired with her courteous "Good-afternoon, Teacher," and her unc-hanged "Good-by, Sadie; I'm got yet that kind feelin'." Truly the "pangs of disprized love" seemed hers.

Several kinds of persuasion were practised in Room 18 during the next five minutes. Then Sadie accepted defeat, faced the inevitable, and began:

"It's like this: I dassent to be glad on Eva. So I want even, I dassent. My mamma has the same mad, und my papa. My mamma she says like this: So my papa gets sooner glad on my uncle she wouldn't to be wifes mit him no more! *Such* is the mad she has!"

"Why?"

"Well. Mine uncle he come out of Russia. From long he come when I was a little bit of baby. Und he didn't to have no money for buy a house. So my papa - he's awful kind - he gives him thousen dollers so he could to buy. Und say, Teacher, what you think? he don't pays it back. It *ain't* polite you takes thousen dollers und don't pays it back."

Sadie's air, as she submitted this rule of social etiquette to Teacher's wider knowledge, was a wondrous thing to see - so deferential was it and yet so assured.

"So my papa he writes a letter on my uncle how he could to pay that thousen dollers. *Goes* months. *Comes* no thousen dollers. So my papa he goes on the lawyer und the lawyer he writes on my uncle a letter how he should to pay. *Goes* months. *Comes* no thousen dollers." At each repetition of these fateful words Sadie shook her serious head, pursed up her rosy mouth, folded her hands resignedly, and sighed deeply. Clearly this was a tale more than twice told, for the voice and manner of Sadie were as the voice and manner of Mrs. Lazarus Gonorowsky, and the recital was plagiarism - masterly and complete.

"And then?" prompted Teacher, lest the conversation languish.

"Well, my papa writes some more a letter on mine uncle. Oh-o-oh, a awful bossy-und-mad letter. All the mad words what my papa knows he writes on mine uncle. Und my mamma she sets by my papa's side und all the mad words what my mamma knows she tells on my papa und he writes them, too, on mine uncle. Mine uncle (that's Eva's papa) could to have a fierce mad sooner he seen that bossy letter. But *goes* two days. *Comes* no thousen dollers."

Here ensued a long and dramatic pause.

"Well, comes no thousen dollers. Comes nothings. On'y by night my mamma she puts me on my bed; when comes my uncle! He comes und makes a knopping on our door. I couldn't to tell even how he makes knopping. I had such a scare I was green on the face, und my heart was going so you could to hear. I'm a nervous child, Missis Bailey, und my face is all times green sooner I gets a scare."

This last observation was a triumph of mimicry, and recalled Mrs. Gonorowsky so vividly as to make her atmosphere of garlic and old furniture quite perceptible. "So my mamma hears how my uncle knopps und says 'Lemme in - lemme in.' She says ('scuse me, Teacher) - she says 'he must be' ('scuse me) 'drunk.' That's how my mamma says.

"So goes my papa by the door und says 'Who stands?' Und my uncle he says 'Lemme in.' So-o-oh my papa he opens the door. Stands my unclemit cheeky looks und he showed a fist on my papa. My papa has a fierce mad sooner he seen that fist - fists is awful cheeky when somebody ain't paid. So my papa he says ('scuse me) - it's fierce how he says, on'y he had a mad over that fist. He says ('scuse me), 'Go to hell!' und my uncle, what ain't paid that thousen dollers, he says just like that to my papa. He says too ('scuse me, Teacher), 'Go to hell!' So-o-oh then my papa hits my uncle (that's Eva's papa), und how my papa is strong I couldn't to tell even. He pulls every morning by the extrasizer, und he's got such a muscles! So he hits my uncle (that's Eva's papa), und my uncle he fall und he fall und he fall - we live by the third floor, und he fall off of the third floor by the street - und even in falling he says like that ('scuse me, Teacher), 'Go to hell! go to hell! go to hell!' Ain't it somethin' fierce how he says? On all the steps he says, 'Go to hell! go to hell! go to hell!'"

Miss Bailey had listened to authoritative lectures upon "The Place and Influence of the Teacher in Community Life," and was debating as to whether she had better inflict her visit of remonstrance upon Mr. Lazarus Gonorowsky, of the powerful and cultivated muscle, or upon Mr. Nathan Gonorowsky, of the deplorable manners, when this opportunity to bring the higher standards of living into the home was taken from her. The house of Gonorowsky, in jagged fragments, was tested as by fire and came forth united.

Eva was absent one morning, and Sadie presented the explanation in a rather dirty envelope:

Dear Miss:

Excuse pliss that Eva Gonarofsky comes not on the school. We was moving und she couldn't to find her clothes.

Yurs Resptphs, Her elders,
Nathan Gonorowsky,
Becky Ganurwoski.

"Is Eva going far away?" asked Teacher. "Will she come to this school any more?"

"Teacher, yiss ma'an, sure she comes; she lives now by my house. My uncle he lives by my house, too. Und my aunt."

"And you're not angry with your cousin anymore?"

"Teacher, no ma'an; I'm loving mit her. She's got on now all mine best clothes the while her mamma buys her new. My aunt buys new clothes, too. Und my uncle."

Sadie reported this shopping epidemic so cheerily that Teacher asked with mild surprise:

"Where are all their old things?"

"Teacher, they're burned. Und my uncle's store und his *all* of goods, und his house und his three sewing machines. All, all burned!"

"Oh, dear me!" said Teacher. "Your poor uncle! Now he can never pay that thousand dollars."

Sadie regarded Teacher with puzzled eyes.

"Sure he pays. He's now 'most as rich like Van'pilt. I guess he's got a hundred dollers. He pays all right, all right, und my papa had a party over him: he had such a awful glad!"

"Glad on your uncle?" cried Teacher, startled into colloquialisms.

"Yiss ma'an. Und my mamma has a glad on Eva's mamma, und my gran'ma has a glad on both of papas und both of mammas, und my gran'pa has a glad just like my gran'ma. All, all glad!"

As Teacher walked towards Grand Street that afternoon, she met a radiant little girl with a small and most unsteady boy in tow. She recognized Eva and surmised the cousin whose coldness had hurt her even unto tears.

"Well, Eva, and what little boy is this?" she asked.

And the beaming and transformed Eva answered:

"It's my little cousin. He's lovin' mit me now. Sadie, too, is lovin'. I take him out the while it's healthy he walks, on'y he ain't so big und he falls. Say, Teacher, it's nice when he falls. I holds him in my hands."

And fall he did. Eva picked him up, greatly to their mutual delight, and explained:

"He's heavy, und my this here arm ain't yet so healthy, but I hold him in my hands the while he's cousins mit me, und over cousins I'm got all times that kind feelin'."

THE USES OF ADVERSITY

"I guess I don't need I should go on the school," announced Algernon Yonowsky.

"I guess you do," said his sister.

"I guess I don't need I should go on the school, neither," remarked Percival.

"You got to go," Leah informed her mutinous brothers. "I got a permit for you from off the Principal; he's friends mit me the while I goes on that school when I was little. You got to go on the school, und you got to stay on the school. It's awful nice how you learn things there."

But the prospect did not appeal to the Yonowsky twins. It seemed to forbode restraint and, during their six tempestuous years, they had followed their own stubborn ways and had accepted neither advice nor rebuke from any man. The evening of the day which had seen their birth had left Leah motherless, and her father broken of heart and of ambition. Since then Mr. Yonowsky had grown daily more silent and morose, and Leah had been less and less able to cope with "them devil boys."

A room high up in a swarming tenement had been the

grave of her youth and pleasure. She was as solitary there as she could have been in a desert, for the neighbours who had known and assisted her in the first years of her bereavement had died or moved to that Mecca of the New World, Harlem. And their successors were not kindly disposed towards a family comprising a silent man, a half-grown girl, and two twin demons who made the block a terror to the nervous and the stairs a menace to the unwary. No one came to gossip with Leah. She was too young to listen understandingly to older women's adventures in sickness or domestic infelicity, and too dispirited to make any show of interest in the toilettes or "affaires" of the younger. For what were incompetent doctors, habit-backed dresses, wavering husbands, or impetuous lovers to Leah Yonowsky, who had assumed all the responsibilities of a woman's life with none of its consolations?

Of course she had, to some extent, failed in the upbringing of her brothers, but she had always looked forward hopefully to the time when they should be old enough to be sent to school. There they should learn, among much other lore, to live up to the names she had selected for them out of the book of love and of adventure which she had been reading at the time of their baptism. During all the years of her enslavement she had been a patron of the nearest public library, and it had been a source of great disappointment to her that Algernon and Percival had made no least attempt to acquire the grace of speech and manner which she had learned to associate with those lordly titles.

And now they were refusing even to approach the Pierian Spring! "I guess I don't go," Algernon was persisting. "I guess I plays on the street."

"Me, too," added Percival. "Patrick Brennan he goes on that school und he gives me over yesterday, a bloody nose. I don' need I should go on no school mit somebody what makes like that mit me."

But with the assistance of the neighbours, the policeman on the beat and the truant officer, they were finally dragged to the halls of learning and delivered into the hands of Miss Bailey, who installed them in widely separated seats and seemed blandly unimpressed by their evident determination to make things unpleasant in Room 18. She met Leah's anticipatory apologies with:

"Of course they'll be good. I shall see that they behave. Yes, I shall see, too, that Patrick Brennan does not fight with Percival. You musn't worry about them any more, but I fear they have made worrying a habit with you. If you will send them to school at a quarter to nine every morning, and at ten minutes to one in the afternoon, I shall do the rest."

And Leah went out into the sunshine free, for the first time in six years. Free to wander through the streets, to do a little desultory shopping, to go down to the river and to watch the workmen driving rivets in the great new bridge. Never had she spent so pleasant a morning, and her heart was full of gratitude and peace when she reflected that hours such as these would henceforth be the order of the day.

The advantages of a free education did not appeal to "them Yonowsky devils." Leah was forced to drag her reluctant charges twice a day to the school-house door - sometimes even up the stairs to Room 18 - and the reports with which Miss Bailey met her were not enthusiastic. Still, Teacher admitted, too much was not to be expected from little boys coming in contact, for the first time, with authority.

"Only send them regularly," she pleaded, "and perhaps they will learn to be happy here." And Leah, in spite of countless obstacles and difficulties, sent them.

They were unusually mutinous one morning, and their dressing had been one long torment to Leah. They persisted in untying strings and unbuttoning buttons. They shrieked, they lay upon the floor and kicked, they spilled coffee upon their "jumpers," and systematically and deliberately reduced their sister to the verge of distraction and of tears. They were already late when she dragged them to the corner of the school, and there they made their last stand by sitting stolidly down upon the pavement.

Leah could not cope with their two rigid little bodies, and, through welling tears of weariness and exasperation, she looked blankly up and down the dingy street for succour. If only her ally, Mr. Brennan, the policeman on the beat, would come! But Mr. Brennan was guarding a Grand Street crossing until such time as the last straggling child should have safely passed the dangers of the horse-cars, and nothing came in answer to Leah's prayer but a push-cart laden with figs and dates and propelled by a tall man, long-coated and fur-capped. His first glance read the tableau, and in an instant he grasped Percival, shook him into animation, threw him through the big door, and turned to reason with Algernon. But that rebel had already seen the error of his ways and was meekly ascending the steps and waving a resigned adieu to his sister. The heavy door clanged. Leah raised grateful eyes to her knight, and the thing was done. For the rest of that day Aaron Kastrinsky sold dates and figs at a reckless discount and dreamed of the fair oval of a girl's face framed in a shawl no more scarlet than her lips, while Leah's heart sang of a youth in a fur cap and a long coat who had been able to "boss them awful boys."

Daily thereafter did Aaron Kastrinsky establish his gay green push-cart outside the school door set apart for the very little boys and drive a half hour's bustling trade ere the children were all housed. And daily two naughty small boys were convoyed to the door by a red-shawled, dark-eyed sister. Very slowly greetings grew from shy glance to shy smile, from swift drooping of the lashes to swift rise of colour, from gentle sweep of eyes to sustained regard, from formal good-morning to protracted chats. But before this happy stage was reached the twins decided that they no longer required safe conduct to the fountain of knowledge, and that Leah's attendance covered them with ridicule in the eyes of more independent spirits. But she refused to relax her vigilance, nay, rather she increased it; for she began to force her mutinous brothers to the synagogue on Sabbath mornings. The twins soon came to associate the vision of Aaron Kastrinsky with the idea of restraint and of stern virtue, for on the way to the synagogue he walked by Leah's side - looking strangely incomplete without his green push-cart - and drove them by the sheer force of his will to walk decorously in front. Decorously, too, he marched them back again, and stood idly talking to Leah at the steps of her tenement while the twins escaped to their enjoyments.

When waiting milk-cans were thrown into cellars, when the wheels of momentarily deserted wagons were loosened, when pushcarts disappeared, when children bent on shopping were waylaid and robbed, when cats were tortured, horses' manes clipped, windows broken, shop-keepers enraged, babies frightened, and pit-falls set upon the stairs, the cry was always, "Them Yonowsky devils." Leah could do nothing with them. Mr. Yonowsky made no effort to control them, and Aaron Kastrinsky was not always there. Not half, not a quarter as often as he wished, for Leah promptly turned away from all his attempts to make her understand how greatly she would gain in peace and comfort if she would but marry him. They would move to a larger flat and he would manage the boys. But Leah's view of life and marriage was tinged with no glory of romance. She had no illusions, no ignorances, and she was afraid, she told her suitor, afraid.

"But of what?" asked the puzzled Aaron. "Thou canst not be afraid of me. Thou knowest how dear thou art to me. What canst thou fear?"

"I'm afraid of being married," was her ultimatum. She confessed that she loved no one else - she had never, poor child, known anyone else to love; she admitted the allurements of the larger flat and the strong hand always ready for the twins, was delighted to go with him to lectures at the Educational Alliance when her father could be aroused to responsible charge of the twins, rejoiced when he prospered in the world and exchanged the push-cart for a permanent fruit-stand - she even assisted at its decoration - but to marry him she was afraid. Yes, she liked him; yes, she would walk with him - and the twins - along Grand Street in the early evening. Yes, she would wear her red dress since he admired it; but to marry him - ah, no! Please, no! she was afraid of being married.

Myra Kelly

Aaron was by birth and in his own country one of the learned class, and he promptly set about supplementing Leah's neglected education. She had lived so solitary a life that her Russian remained pure and soft and was quite distinct from the mixture of Yiddish, German, English, and slang which her neighbours spoke. English, which she read easily, she spoke rarely and haltingly, and Jewish in a prettily pedantic manner, learned from her mother, whose father had been a Rabbi. Aaron lent her books in these three languages, which straightway carried her into strange and glorious worlds. Occasionally the twins stole and sold the books, but their enlightenment remained. To supplement the reading he took her to lectures and to night schools, and thus one evening they listened to an illustrated "talk" on "Contagion and Its Causes." There had been an epidemic of smallpox in the quarter and Panic was abroad. Parents who spoke no English fought wildly with ambulance surgeons who spoke no Jewish, and refused to entrust the sufferers to the care of the Board of Health. Many disturbances resulted and the authorities arranged that, in all the missions, night schools, and settlements of the East Side, reassuring lecturers should spread abroad the folly of resistance, the joys of hospital life, the surety of recovery in the arms of the board, with a few remarks upon the sources of contagion.

Leah and Aaron listened to one of the most calming of these orators. The lecturer spoke with such feeling - and such stereopticon slides - that smallpox, scarlet fever, measles, and diphtheria seemed the "open sesame" to bliss unutterable, and the source of these talismans rather to be sought for diligently than shunned. "Didst hear?" Leah asked Aaron as they went home. "For a redness on the skin one may stay in bed for a week and rest."

"Ay, but one is sick," said Aaron sagely.

"Not if one goes where the gentleman said. One lies in bed for a week - three weeks - and there be ladies who wait on one, and one rests - all days one rests. And there be no twins. Think of it, Aaron! rest and no twins!"

A few days later she climbed home after a morning's shopping to find Algernon, heavy of eye and red of face, crouched near the locked door with a whimper in his voice and a card in his hand.

"I'm got somethin'," he announced, with the pride of the invalid.

"Where didst get it?" asked Leah, automatically; she was accustomed to brazen admission of guilt.

"Off of a boy at school."

"Thou wilt steal once too often," his sister admonished him. "Go now, confess to Miss Bailey, and return what thou hast taken."

"The boy has it too," retorted Algernon. "It's a sickness - a taking sickness; und comes a man und gives me a card und says I should come by my house; I'm sick."

Leah gazed on the card in despairing envy. She had hopefully searched her person for rash or redness, thinking thereby to achieve a ticket to that promised land where beautiful ladies - as the stereopticon had shown - sat graciously waving fans beside a smooth, white bed whereon one lay and rested: only rested: quiet day after quiet day. There had been no twins in her imaginings, yet here was Algernon already set upon the way; Algernon, who would be naughty in that blissful place, and who might even "talk sassy" to the beautiful ladies. Slow tears of disappointment grew under Leah's heavy lids and splashed upon the coveted ticket. And the doctor from the Board of Health, come to verify the more superficial examination of his colleague, misguidedly launched forth upon a resume of the reassuring lectures.

"You mustn't cry," he remonstrated. "It's only measles and he won't be very sick. Why, you might keep him here, and I could send you a nurse to show you how to take care of him if it weren't for that butcher shop on the ground floor. But he'll be all right. Don't cry."

In a short space the house of Yonowsky was bereft of its more noisy son, and peace reigned. Percival went lonely and early to bed. Leah sat late on the steps with Aaron, and, on the next morning, Percival duplicated the redness, the diagnosis, and the departure of his brother, and Leah came into her own.

Then were the days wondrous long. There was time for all the pleasures from which she had been so long debarred. Time to read, time to sew, time to pay and to receive shy, short morning calls, time to scrub and polish until her room shone, time for experiments in cookery, time to stretch her father's wages to undreamed-of lengths, even time so to cheer and wheedle Mr. Yonowsky that she dared to ask his permission to bring Aaron up to her spotless domain. And Aaron, with a thumping of the hearts not due entirely to the height and steepness of the stairs, came formally to call upon his young divinity. The visit was a great success. Mr. Yonowsky blossomed under the sun of Aaron's deference and learning into an expansiveness which amazed his daughter, and the men discussed the law, the scriptures, the election, the Czar, nihilism, socialism, the tariff, and the theatre. But here Mr. Yonowsky lapsed into gloom. He had not visited a theatre for seven years - not since his wife's death.

"And Miss Leah?" Aaron questioned.

"Never, oh, never!" she breathed resignedly, yet so longingly that Aaron then and there arranged that he and she and Mr. Yonowsky should visit the Thalia Theatre on the following night. And Leah, with the glad and new assurance that the boys were safe, fell into happy devisings of a suitable array. When young Kastrinsky left after formal and prescribed adieus to his hostess, he dragged his host out to listen to a campaign speech.

During the weeks that followed, even Mr. Yonowsky came to see the sweet uses of the Board of Health and to ponder long and deeply upon the nature of the "taking sickness." No longer forced to do perpetual, though ineffective, sentinel duty, he gradually resumed his place in the world of men and spent placid evenings at the synagogue, the Educational Alliance, the theatre, and the East Side Democratic Union. Leah bore him company at the theatre when she might, and Aaron followed Leah until parental pride swelled high under Mr. Yonowsky's green Prince Albert coat. For well he saw the looks of admiration which were turned upon his daughter as she sat by his side and consumed cold pink lemonade.

He received two of the roundabout proposals which etiquette demands, and began to gather a dowry for Leah and to recall extraordinary outstanding securities to that end. But, before these things were accomplished, his sons and his troubles returned upon him. With renewed energy, stimulated imagination, and enriched profanity, "them Yonowsky devils" came home, and their reign of mischief set in afresh.

They had always been unruly; they were utterly unmanageable now. Daily was Leah summoned to the big red school-house by the long-suffering Miss Bailey, and nightly was Mr. Yonowsky forced to cancel engagements at club or synagogue and to stay at home to "explanation them boys" to outraged neighbours.

Aaron could still control them, but he was never brought upstairs now. How could Leah expect him to enjoy conversations carried on amid the yells of Algernon and Percival in freedom, or their shrieks in durance?

The twins came home one noontime full of gossip and excitement. They clamoured over their cabbage soup that a classmate of theirs, one Isidore Belchatosky, had "a sickness - a taking sickness, what he took from off his sister Sadie."

"Is it a bad sickness?" asked the father.

"Somethin' fierce!" Percival assured him. "Pimples stands on his face, und he *says* he's got 'em everywheres, but I guess maybe he lies. He says it's a chicken sickness what he has. Mit pimples everywheres!"

"You don't know no names from sicknesses," Algernon broke in contemptuously. "It ain't the chicken sickness. It's the chicken puffs."

"Where is his house?" asked Leah eagerly. And she joyously despatched the twins with kind inquiries and proffers to sit with the sufferer; for had not the prophesying gentleman explained that there was no surer way of attaining to hospital tickets than by speech and contact with one who had already "arrived"? And Algernon and Percival, spurred on by the allurement of the "pimples everywheres," pressed past all barriers and outposts until they feasted their eyes upon the neatly spotted Izzie, who proudly proved his boast of the "everywheres" and the exceeding puffiness of the chicken puffs.

Two weeks later the little emissaries of love were in sorry case. The "pimples everywheres" appeared, the ambulance reappeared, the twins disappeared. The cleaning and polishing were resumed, Aaron invited to supper, Mr. Yonowsky pledged to deliver a lecture on "The Southern Negro and the Ballot," and a stew of the strongest elements set to simmer on the stove.

Leah had learned the path to freedom and trod it with a light heart. Algernon and Percival enjoyed a long succession of diseases, contagious and infectious, and each attack meant a holiday of varying but always of considerable length. Under ordinary conditions Leah might have been forced to nurse her brothers through their less serious disorders, but there was a butcher shop on the ground floor of the Yonowsky tenement, and the by-laws of the Board of Health decreed that, such being the case, the children should be removed for nearly all the ills to which young and ill-nourished flesh is heir.

"Them Yonowsky devils" became only visitors to their native block, but since they returned after each retirement more unruly and outrageous, they were not deeply mourned. Only the butcher objected, because his store was occasionally quarantined when Leah had achieved some very virulent excuse for summoning the ambulance and shipping her responsibilities. Mr. Yonowsky was puzzled but grateful, and Aaron was grateful too.

Month after month went by and the twins had exhausted the lists of the lecturer and had enjoyed several other ailments, when Leah and her father went to bring them home from their typhoid-fever holiday.

"You've been having a hard time with these boys," the man at the desk said kindly. "The worst luck I ever knew in the many years I've been here. But they're all right now. They've had everything on the list except water on the brain and elephantiasis, and they can't get them."

"But some what they had they could some more get," Leah suggested in the English she so rarely used.

"I think not," the official answered cheeringly. "They hardly ever do. No, I guess you'll be able to keep them at home now. Good luck to you!"

But it was bad luck, the worst of luck. Mr. Yonowsky's public spirit died within his breast; Leah's coquetry vanished before a future unrelieved by visits from the black and friendly ambulance, and when Aaron climbed the well-known stairs that evening he heard, while he was yet two floors short of his destination, the shrieks of the twins, the smashing of crockery, and the grumbling of the neighbours. Suddenly a little figure darted upon him and Leah was in his arms.

"Aaron," she sobbed. "Oh, Aaron, mine heart it breaks. There ain't no more taking sicknesses in all the world. So says the gentleman."

"My golden one," said Aaron, who was a bit of a philosopher; "all good things come to an end except only Love. And the twins have had taking sicknesses in great and unheard-of numbers."

"But now they are more than ever bad. I can do nothing with them and I am afraid of them. In hospitals, where one is very happy, one grows very big, and the twins are no longer little boys."

"If you marry me - " Aaron began.

"You will love me always?"

"Yea, mine gold."

"And for me you will boss them twins'?"

"Yea, verily, for thee I will boss the twins."

And the betrothal of Leah Yonowsky to Aaron Kastrinsky was signed and sealed immediately.

A CHRISTMAS PRESENT FOR A LADY

It was the week before Christmas, and the First-Reader Class had, almost to a man, decided on the gifts to be lavished on "Teacher." She was quite unprepared for any such observance on the part of her small adherents, for her first study of the roll-book had shown her that its numerous Jacobs, Isidores, and Rachels belonged to a class to which Christmas Day was much as other days. And so she went serenely on her way, all unconscious of the swift and strict relation between her manner and her chances. She was, for instance, the only person in the room who did not know that her criticism of Isidore Belchatosky's hands and face cost her a tall "three for ten cents" candlestick and a plump box of candy.

But Morris Mogilewsky, whose love for Teacher was far greater than the combined loves of all the other children, had as yet no present to bestow. That his "kind feeling" should be without proof when the lesser loves of Isidore Wishnewsky, Sadie Gonorowsky, and Bertha Binderwitz were taking the tangible but surprising forms which were daily exhibited to his confidential gaze, was more than he could bear. The knowledge saddened all his hours and was the more maddening because it could in no wise be shared by Teacher, who noticed his altered bearing and tried with all sorts of artful beguilements to make him happy and at ease. But her efforts served only to increase his unhappiness and his love. And he loved her! Oh, how he loved her! Since first his dreading eyes had clung for a breath's space to her "like man's shoes" and had then crept timidly upward past a black skirt, a "from silk" apron, a red "jumper," and "from gold" chain to her "light face," she had been mistress of his heart of hearts. That was more than three months ago. And well he remembered the day!

His mother had washed him horribly, and had taken him into the big, red school-house, so familiar from the outside, but so full of unknown terrors within. After his dusty little shoes had stumbled over the threshold he had passed from ordeal to ordeal until at last he was torn in mute and white-faced despair from his mother's skirts.

He was then dragged through long halls and up tall stairs by a large boy, who spoke to him disdainfully as "greenie," and cautioned him as to the laying down softly and taking up gently of those poor dusty shoes, so that his spirit was quite broken and his nerves were all unstrung when he was pushed into a room full of bright sunshine and of children who laughed at his frightened little face. The sunshine smote his timid eyes, the laughter smote his timid heart, and he turned to flee. But the door was shut, the large boy gone, and despair took him for its own.

Down upon the floor he dropped, and wailed, and wept, and kicked. It was then that he heard, for the first time the voice which now he loved. A hand was forced between his aching body and the floor, and the voice said: "Why, my dear little chap, you mustn't cry like that. What's the matter?"

The hand was gentle and the question kind, and these, combined with a faint perfume suggestive of drug stores and barber shops - but nicer than either - made him uncover his hot little face. Kneeling beside him was a lady, and he forced his eyes to that perilous ascent; from shoes to skirt, from skirt to jumper, from jumper to face, they trailed in dread uncertainty, but at the face they stopped. They had found - rest.

Morris allowed himself to be gathered into the lady's arms and held upon her knee, and when his sobs no longer rent the very foundations of his pink and wide-spread tie, he answered her question in a voice as soft as his eyes, and as gently sad.

"I ain't so big, und I don't know where is my mamma."

So, having cast his troubles on the shoulders of the lady, he had added his throbbing head to the burden, and from that safe retreat had enjoyed his first day at school immensely.

Thereafter he had been the first to arrive every morning, and the last to leave every afternoon; and under the care of Teacher, his liege lady, he had grown in wisdom and love and happiness. But the greatest of these was love. And now, when the other boys and girls were planning surprises and gifts of price for Teacher, his hands were as empty as his heart was full. Appeal to his mother met with denial prompt and energetic.

"For what you go und make, over Christmas, presents? You ain't no Krisht; you should better have no kind feelings over Krishts, neither; your papa could to have a mad."

"Teacher ain't no Krisht," said Morris stoutly; "all the other fellows buys her presents, und I'm loving mit her too; it's polite I gives her presents the while I'm got such a kind feeling over her."

"Well, we ain't got no money for buy nothings," said Mrs. Mogilewsky sadly. "No money, und your papa, he has all times a scare he shouldn't to get no more, the while the boss" - and here followed incomprehensible, but depressing, financial details, until the end of the interview found Morris and his mother sobbing and rocking in one another's arms. So Morris was helpless, his mother poor, and Teacher all unknowing.

And the great day, the Friday before Christmas came, and the school was, for the first half hour, quite mad. Doors opened suddenly and softly to admit small persons, clad in wondrous ways and bearing wondrous parcels. Room 18, generally so placid and so peaceful, was a howling wilderness full of brightly coloured, quickly changing groups of children, all whispering, all gurgling, and all hiding queer bundles. A newcomer invariably caused a diversion; the assembled multitude, athirst for novelty, fell upon him and clamoured for a glimpse of his bundle and a statement of its price.

Teacher watched in dumb amaze. What could be the matter with the children, she wondered. They could not have guessed the shrouded something in the corner to be a Christmas-tree. What made them behave so queerly, and why did they look so strange? They seemed to have grown stout in a single night, and Teacher, as she noted this, marvelled greatly. The explanation was simple, though it came in alarming form. The sounds of revelry were pierced by a long, shrill yell, and a pair of agitated legs sprang suddenly into view between two desks. Teacher, rushing to the rescue, noted that the legs formed the unsteady stem of an upturned mushroom of brown flannel and green braid, which she recognized as the outward seeming of her cherished Bertha Binderwitz; and yet, when the desks were forced to disgorge their prey, the legs restored to their normal position were found to support a fat child - and Bertha was best described as "skinny" - in a dress of the Stuart tartan tastefully trimmed with purple. Investigation proved that Bertha's accumulative taste in dress was an established custom. In nearly all cases the glory of holiday attire was hung upon the solid foundation of every-day clothes as bunting is hung upon a building. The habit was economical of time, and produced a charming embonpoint.

Teacher, too, was more beautiful than ever. Her dress was blue, and "very long down, like a lady," with bands of silk and scraps of lace distributed with the eye of art. In her hair she wore a bow of what Sadie Gonorowsky, whose father "worked by fancy goods," described as black "from plush ribbon - costs ten cents."

Isidore Belchatosky, relenting, was the first to lay tribute before Teacher. He came forward with a sweet smile and a tall candlestick - the candy had gone to its long home - and Teacher, for a moment, could not be made to understand that all that length of bluish-white china was really hers "for keeps."

"It's to-morrow holiday," Isidore assured her; "and we gives you presents, the while we have a kind feeling. Candlesticks could to cost twenty-five cents."

"It's a lie. Three for ten," said a voice in the

background, but Teacher hastened to respond to Isidore's test of her credulity:

"Indeed, they could. This candlestick could have cost fifty cents, and it's just what I want. It is very good of you to bring me a present."

"You're welcome," said Isidore, retiring; and then, the ice being broken, the First-Reader Class in a body rose to cast its gifts on Teacher's desk, and its arms around Teacher's neck.

Nathan Horowitz presented a small cup and saucer; Isidore Applebaum bestowed a large calendar for the year before last; Sadie Gonorowsky brought a basket containing a bottle of perfume, a thimble, and a bright silk handkerchief; Sarah Schrodsky offered a pen-wiper and a yellow celluloid collar-button, and Eva Kidansky gave an elaborate nasal douche, under the pleasing delusion that it was an atomizer.

Once more sounds of grief reached Teacher's ears. Rushing again to the rescue, she threw open the door and came upon Woe personified. Eva Gonorowsky, her hair in wildest disarray, her stocking fouled, ungartered, and down-gyved to her ankle, appeared before her teacher. She bore all the marks of Hamlet's excitement, and many more, including a tear-stained little face and a gilt saucer clasped to a panting breast.

"Eva, my dearest Eva, what's happened to you *now*?" asked Teacher, for the list of ill-chances which had befallen this one of her charges was very long. And Eva's wail was that a boy, a very big boy, had stolen her golden cup "what I had for you by present," and had left her only the saucer and her undying love to bestow.

Before Eva's sobs had quite yielded to Teacher's arts, Jacob Spitsky pressed forward with a tortoise-shell comb of terrifying aspect and hungry teeth, and an air showing forth a determination to adjust it in its destined place. Teacher meekly bowed her head; Jacob forced his offering into her long-suffering hair, and then retired with the information, "Costs fifteen cents, Teacher," and the courteous phrase - by etiquette prescribed - "Wish you health to wear it." He was plainly a hero, and was heard remarking to less favoured admirers that "Teacher's hair is awful softy, and smells off of perfumery."

Here a big boy, a very big boy, entered hastily. He did not belong to Room 18, but he had long known Teacher. He had brought her a present; he wished her a Merry Christmas. The present, when produced, proved to be a pretty gold cup, and Eva Gonorowsky, with renewed emotion, recognized the boy as her assailant and the cup as her property. Teacher was dreadfully embarrassed; the boy not at all so. His policy was simple and entire denial, and in this he persevered, even after Eva's saucer had unmistakably proclaimed its relationship to the cup.

Meanwhile the rush of presentation went steadily on. Other cups and saucers came in wild profusion. The desk was covered with them, and their wrappings of purple tissue paper required a monitor's whole attention. The soap, too, became urgently perceptible. It was of all sizes, shapes and colours, but of uniform and dreadful power of perfumes Teacher's eyes filled with tears - of gratitude - as each new piece or box was pressed against her nose, and Teacher's mind was full of wonder as to what she could ever do with all of it. Bottles of perfume vied with one another and with the all-pervading soap until the air was heavy and breathing grew labourious. But pride swelled the hearts of the assembled multitude. No other Teacher had so many helps to the toilet. None other was so beloved.

Teacher's aspect was quite changed, and the "blue long down like a lady dress" was almost hidden by the offerings she had received. Jacob's comb had two massive and bejewelled rivals in the "softy hair." The front of the dress, where aching or despondent heads were wont to rest, glittered with campaign buttons of American celebrities, beginning with James G. Blaine and extending into modern history as far as Patrick Divver, Admiral Dewey, and Captain Dreyfus. Outside the blue belt was a white one, nearly clean, and bearing in "sure 'nough golden words" the curt, but stirring, invitation, "Remember the Maine." Around the neck were three chaplets of beads, wrought by chubby fingers and embodying much love, while the waist-line was further adorned by tiny and beribboned aprons. Truly, it was a day of triumph.

When the waste-paper basket had been twice filled with wrappings and twice emptied; when order was emerging out of chaos; when the Christmas-tree had been disclosed and its treasures distributed, a timid hand was laid on Teacher's knee and a plaintive voice whispered, "Say, Teacher, I got something for you;" and Teacher turned quickly to see Morris, her dearest boy charge, with his poor little body showing quite plainly between his shirt-waist buttons and through the gashes he called pockets. This was his ordinary costume, and the funds of the house of Mogilewsky were evidently unequal to an outer layer of finery.

"Now, Morris dear," said Teacher, "you shouldn't have troubled to get me a present; you know you and I are such good friends that - "

"Teacher, yiss ma'an," Morris interrupted, in a bewitching and rising inflection of his soft and plaintive voice. "I know you got a kind feeling by me, and I couldn't to tell even how I got a kind feeling by you. Only it's about that kind feeling I should give you a present. I didn't" - with a glance at the crowded desk - "I didn't to have no soap nor no perfumery, and my mamma she couldn't to buy none by the store; but, Teacher, I'm got something awful nice for you by present."

"And what is it, deary?" asked the already rich and gifted young person. "What is my new present?"

"Teacher, it's like this: I don't know; I ain't so big like I could to know" - and, truly, God pity him! he was passing small - "it ain't for boys - it's for ladies. Over yesterday on the night comes my papa to my house, und he gives my mamma the present. Sooner she looks on it, sooner she has a awful glad; in her eyes stands tears, und she says, like that - out of Jewish - 'Thanks,' un' she kisses my papa a kiss. Und my papa, *how* he is polite! he says - out of Jewish too - 'You're welcome, all right,' un' he kisses my mamma a kiss. So my mamma, she sets und looks on the present, und all the time she looks she has a glad over it. Und I didn't to have no soap, so you could to have the present."

"But did your mother say I might?"

"Teacher, no ma'an; she didn't say like that, und she didn't to say *not* like that. She didn't to know. But it's for ladies, un' Ididn't to have no soap. You could to look on it. It ain't for boys."

And here Morris opened a hot little hand and disclosed a tightly folded pinkish paper. As Teacher read it he watched her with eager, furtive eyes, dry and bright, until hers grew suddenly moist, when his promptly followed suit. As she looked down at him, he made his moan once more:

"It's for ladies, und I didn't to have no soap."

"But, Morris, dear," cried Teacher unsteadily, laughing a little, and yet not far from tears, "this is ever so much nicer than soap - a thousand times better than perfume; and you're quite right, it is for ladies, and I never had one in all my life before. I am so very thankful."

"You're welcome, all right. That's how my papa says; it's polite," said Morris proudly. And proudly he took his place among the very little boys, and loudly he joined in the ensuing song. For the rest of that exciting day he was a shining point of virtue in the rest of that confused class. And at three o'clock he was at Teacher's desk again, carrying on the conversation as if there had been no interruption.

"Und my mamma," he said insinuatingly - "she kisses my papa a kiss."

"Well?" said Teacher.

"Well," said Morris, "you ain't never kissed me a kiss, und I seen how you kissed Eva Gonorowsky. I'm loving mit you too. Why don't you never kiss me a kiss?"

"Perhaps," suggested Teacher mischievously, "perhaps it ain't for boys."

But a glance at her "light face," with its crown of surprising combs, reassured him.

"Teacher, yiss ma'an; it's for boys," he cried as he felt her arms about him, and saw that in her eyes, too, "stands tears."

"It's polite you kisses me a kiss over that for ladies' present."

Late that night Teacher sat in her pretty room - for she was, unofficially, a greatly pampered young person - and reviewed her treasures. She saw that they were very numerous, very touching, very whimsical, and very precious. But above all the rest she cherished a frayed and pinkish paper, rather crumpled and a little soiled. For it held the love of a man and a woman and a little child, and the magic of a home, for Morris Mogilewsky's Christmas present for ladies was the receipt for a month's rent for a room on the top floor of a Monroe Street tenement.

LOVE AMONG THE BLACKBOARDS

An organized government requires a cabinet, and, during the first weeks of her reign over Room 18, Miss Bailey set about providing herself with aides and advisors. She made, naturally, some fatal and expensive mistakes, as when she entrusted the class pencils to the care of one of the Yonowsky twins who, promptly falling ill of scarlet fever and imparting it to his brother, reduced the First-Reader Class to writing with coloured chalk.

But gradually from the rank and file of candidates, from the well-meaning but clumsy; from the competent but dishonest; from the lazy and from the rash, she selected three loyal and devoted men to share her task of ruling. They were Morris Mogilewsky, Prime Minister and Monitor of the Gold-Fish Bowl; Nathan Spiderwitz, Councillor of the Exchequer and Monitor of Window Boxes; and Patrick Brennan, Commander-in-Chief of the Forces and Leader of the Line.

The members of this cabinet, finding themselves raised to such high places by the pleasure of their sovereign, kept watchful eyes upon her. For full well they knew that cruelest of all the laws of the Board of Education, which decrees: "That the marriage of a female teacher shall constitute resignation." This ruling had deprived them of a Kindergarten teacher of transcendent charm and had made them as watchful of Miss Bailey as a bevy of maiden aunts could have been. Losing her they would lose love and power, and love and power are sweet.

Morris was the first to discover definite grounds for uneasiness. He met his cherished Miss Bailey walking across Grand Street on a rainy morning, and the umbrella which was protecting her beloved head was held by a tall stranger in a long and baggy coat. After circling incredulously about this tableau, Morris dashed off to report to his colleagues. He found Patrick and Nathan in the midst of an exciting game of craps, but his pattering feet warned them of danger, so they pocketed their dice and turned to hear his news.

"Say," he panted; "I seen Teacher mit a man."

"No!" said Patrick, aghast.

"It's a lie!" cried Nathan; "it's a lie!"

"No; it's no lie," said Morris, with a sob half of breathlessness and half of sorrow; "I seen her for sure. Und the man carries umbrellas over her mit loving looks."

"Ah, g'wan," drawled Patrick; "you're crazy. You don't know what you're talking about."

"Sure do I," cried Morris. "I had once a auntie what was loving mit a awful stylish salesman - he's now floorwalkers - und I see how they makes."

"Well," said Patrick, "I had a sister Mary and she married the milkman, so I know, too. But umbrellas doesn't mean much."

"But the loving looks," Morris insisted. "My auntie makes such looks on the salesman - he's now floorwalkers - und sooner she marries mit him."

"Say, Patrick," suggested Nathan; "I'll tell you what to do. You ask her if she's goin' to get married."

"Naw," said Patrick. "Let Morris ask her. She'd tell him before she'd tell any of us. She's been soft on him ever since Christmas. Say, Morris, do you hear? You've got to ask Teacher if she's going to get married."

"Oo-o-oh! I dassent. It ain't polite how you says," cried Morris in his shocked little voice. "It *ain't* polite you asks like that. It's fierce."

"Well, you've got to do it, anyway," said Patrick darkly, "and you've got to do it soon, and you've got to let us hear you."

"It's fierce," protested Morris, but he was overruled by the dominant spirit of Patrick Brennan, that grandson of the kings of Munster and son of the policeman on the beat. His opportunity found him on the very next morning. Isidore Wishnewsky, the gentlest of gentle children, came to school wearing his accustomed air of melancholy shot across with a tender pride. His subdued "Good morning" was accompanied with much strenuous exertion directed, apparently, to the removal and exhibition of a portion of his spine. After much wriggling he paused long enough to say:

"Teacher, what you think? I'm got a present for you,"

and then recommenced his search in another layer of his many flannels. His efforts being at length crowned with success, he drew forth and spread before Teacher's admiring eyes a Japanese paper napkin.

"My sister," he explained. "She gets it to a weddinge."

"Oh, Isidore," cried the flattered Teacher; "it's very pretty, isn't it?"

"Teacher - yiss ma'an," gurgled Isidore. "It's stylish. You could to look on how stands birds on it and flowers. Mine sister she gives it to me und I gives it to you. *I* don't need it. She gives me all times something the while she's got such a kind feelin' over me. She goes all times on weddinges. Most all her younge lady friends gettin' married; ain't it funny?"

At the fateful word "married," the uneasy cabinet closed in about Teacher. Their three pairs of eyes clung to her face as Isidore repeated:

"All gettin' married. Ain't it funny?"

"Well, no, dear," answered Teacher musingly. "You know nearly all young ladies do it."

Patrick took a pin from Teacher's desk and kneeled to tie his shoe-string. When he rose the point of the pin projected half an inch beyond the frayed toe of his shoe, and he was armed. Morris was most evidently losing courage - he was indeed trying to steal away when Patrick pressed close beside him and held him to his post.

"Teacher," said Isidore suddenly, as a dreadful thought

struck him, "be you a lady or be you a girl?"

And Teacher, being of Hibernian ancestry, answered one question with another:

"Which do you think, Isidore?"

"Well," Isidore answered, "I don't know be you a forsure lady or be you a forsure girl. You wears your hair so tucked up und your dress so long down like you was a lady, but you laffs und tells us stories like you was a girl. I don't know."

Clearly this was Morris's opening. Patrick pierced his soul with a glance of scorn and simultaneously buried the pin in his quaking leg. Thus encouraged, Morris rushed blindly into the conversation with:

"Say, Teacher, Miss Bailey, be *you* goin' to get married?" and then dropped limply against her shoulder.

The question was not quite new to Teacher and, as she bestowed Morris more comfortably on her knee, she pondered once again. She knew that, for the present, her lines had fallen in very pleasant places, and she felt no desire to change to pastures new. And yet - and yet -. The average female life is long, and a Board, however thoughtful as to salary and pension, is an impersonal lord and master, and remote withal. So she answered quite simply, with her cheek against the boy's:

"Well, perhaps so, Morris. Perhaps I shall, some day."

"Teacher, no ma'an, Miss Bailey!" wailed the Monitor

of the Gold-Fish. "Don't you go and get married mit nobody. So you do you couldn't be Teacher by us no more, and you're a awful nice teacher by little boys. You ain't *too* big. Und say, we'd feel terrible bad the while you goes and gets married mit somebody - terrible bad."

"Should you really, now?" asked Teacher, greatly pleased. "Well, dear, I too should be lonely without you."

Here Isidore Wishnewsky, who considered this conversation as his cherished own, and saw it being torn from him, determined to outdo the favoured Morris as a squire of dames.

"Teacher, yiss ma'an," he broke in. "We'd all feel terrible the while we ain't got you by teacher. All the boys und all the girls they says like this - it's the word in the yard - we ain't never had a teacher smells so nice like you."

While Teacher was in the lenient mood, resulting from this astounding tribute, Nathan forged yet another chain for her securing.

"Teacher," said he, "you wouldn't never go and get married mit nobody 'out saying nothing to somebody, would you?"

"Indeed, no, my dear," Miss Bailey assured him. "When I marry, you and Patrick and Morris shall be ushers - monitors, you know. Now are you happy, you funny little chaps?"

"Teacher, yiss ma'an," Morris sighed, as the bell rang

sharply, and the aloof and formal exercise of the assembly room began.

Some days later Teacher arranged to go to a reception, and as she did not care to return to her home between work and play, she appeared at school in rather festive array. Room 18 was delighted with its transformed ruler, but to the board of monitors this glory of raiment brought nothing but misery. Every twist in the neat coiffure, every fold of the pretty dress, every rustle of the invisible silk, every click of the high heels, meant the coming abdication of Teacher and the disbanding of her cabinet. Just so had Patrick's sister Mary looked on the day she wed the milkman. Just such had been the outward aspect of Morris's auntie on the day of her union to the promising young salesman who was now a floorwalker and Morris's Uncle Ikey.

Momentarily they expected some word of farewell - perhaps even an ice-cream party - but Teacher made no sign. They decided that she was reserving her last words for their private ear and were greatly disconcerted to find themselves turned out with the common herd at three o'clock. With heavy hearts they followed the example of Mary's little lamb and waited patiently about till Teacher did appear. When she came she was more wonderful than ever, in a long and billowy boa and a wide and billowy hat. She had seemed in a breathless hurry while up in Room 18, but now she stood quite placidly in a group of her small adherents on the highest of the school-house steps. And the cabinet, waiting gloomily apart, only muttered, "I told ye so," and "It must be a awful kind feeling," when the tall stranger came swinging upon the scene. When Teacher's eyes fell upon him she began to force her way through her clinging court, and when he was half way up the steps she was half way down. As they met he drew from his pocket a hand and the violets it held and Teacher was still adjusting the flowers in her jacket when she passed her lurking staff. "I didn't expect you at all," she was saying. "You know it was not a really definite arrangement, and men hate receptions."

A big voice replied in a phrase which Morris identified as having been prominent in the repertoire of the enamoured salesman - now a floorwalker - and Teacher with her companion turned to cross the street. Her heels clicked for yet a moment and the deserted cabinet knew that all was over.

The gloom obscuring Patrick's spirit on that evening was of so deep a dye that Mrs. Brennan diagnosed it as the first stage of "a consumption." She administered simple remedies and warm baths with perseverance, but without effect. And more potent to cure than bath or bottle was the sight of Teacher on the next morning in her accustomed clothes and place.

The Board of Monitors had hardly recovered from this panic when another alarming symptom appeared. Miss Bailey began to watch for letters, and large envelopes began to reward her watchfulness. Daily was Patrick sent to the powers that were to demand a letter, and daily he carried one, and a sorely heavy heart, back to his sovereign. In exactly the same sweetly insistent way had he been sent many a time and oft to seek tidings of the laggard milkman. His colleagues, when he laid these facts before them, were of the opinion that things looked very dark for Teacher. Said Nathan:

"You know how she says we should be monitors on

her weddinge? Well, it could to be lies. She marries maybe already."

Patrick promptly knocked the Monitor of Window Boxes down upon the rough asphalt of the yard and kicked him.

"Miss Bailey's no sneak," he cried hotly. "If she was married she'd just as lief go and tell."

"Well," Morris began, "I had once a auntie - "

"Your auntie makes me sick," snapped Patrick. But Morris went on quite undisturbedly:

"I had once a auntie und she had awful kind feelings over a stylish floorwalker, und he was loving mit her. So-o-oh! They marries! Und they don't say nothings to nobody. On'y the stylish floor walker he writes on my auntie whole bunches of lovin' letters."

"She ain't married," Patrick reiterated. "She ain't."

"Well, she will be," muttered Nathan vindictively. "Und the new teacher will lick you the while you fights. It's fierce how you make me biles on my bones. Think shame."

When the ruffled Monitor of the Window Boxes had been soothed by the peaceful Guardian of the Gold-Fish, the cabinet held council. Nathan suggested that it might be possible to bribe the interloper. They would give him their combined wealth and urge him to turn his eyes upon Miss Blake, whose room was across the hall. She was very big and would do excellently well for him, whereas she was entirely too long and too wide for them.

Morris maintained that Teacher might be held by gratitude. A list should be made out, and, each in turn, a child a day, should give her a present.

Patrick listened to these ideas in deep and restive disgust. He urged instant and copious bloodshed. His big brother's gang could "let daylight into the dude" with enjoyment and despatch. They would watch him ceaselessly and they would track him down.

The watching was an easy matter, for Teacher, in common with the majority of rulers, lived much in the public eye. The stranger was often detected prowling in her vicinity. He even began to bring her to school in the mornings, and on these occasions there were always violets in her coat. He used to appear at luncheon time and vanish with her. He used to come in the afternoon and have tea in Room 18 with two other teachers and with Teacher. The antagonism of the Monitor of Gold Fish became so marked that Miss Bailey was forced to remonstrate.

"Morris, dear," she began one afternoon, when they were alone together, "you were very rude to Doctor Ingraham yesterday. I can't allow you to stay here with me if you're going to behave so badly. You sulked horribly and you slammed the door against his foot. Of course it was an accident, but how would you feel, Morris, if you had hurt him?"

"Glad," said the Monitor of the Gold-Fish savagely. "Glad."

"Morris! What do you mean by saying such a thing?

I'm ashamed of you. Why should you want to hurt a friend of mine?"

"Don't you be friends mit him!" cried Morris, deserting his fish and throwing himself upon his teacher. "Don't you do it, Teacher Missis Bailey. He ain't no friends for a lady." And then, in answer to Teacher's stare of blank surprise, he went on:

"My mamma she seen him by your side und she says - I got to tell you in whispering how she says."

Teacher bent her head and Morris whispered in an awe-struck voice:

"My mamma says she like that: 'He could to be a Krisht,'" and then drew back to study Teacher's consternation. But she seemed quite calm. Perhaps she had already faced the devastating fact, for she said:

"Yes, I know he's a Christian. I'm not afraid of them. Are you?"

"Teacher, no ma'an, Missis Bailey, I ain't got no scare over Krishts, on'y they ain't no friends for ladies. My papa says like that on my auntie, und my auntie she's married now mit a stylish floorwalker. We'm got a Krisht in our house for boarder, so I know. But *you* couldn't to know 'bout Krishts."

"Yes, I do. They're very nice people."

"No ma'an," said Morris gently. And then still more courteously: "It's a lie. You couldn't to know about Krishts."

"But I do know all about them, Morris dear. I'm a Christian."

Again Morris remembered his manners. Again he replied in his courtly phrase:

"It's a lie." As he said it, with a bewitching rising inflection, it was almost a caress. "It's a lie. Teacher fools. You couldn't to be no Krisht. You ain't got no looks off of Krishts."

Teacher was mildly surprised. She was as Irish as Patrick Brennan and, in her own way, she looked it. Truly her eyes were brown, but the face and the faith of her fathers were still strongly hers. Morris, meanwhile, examined his sovereign with admiring eyes. He could well understand the heart of that Krisht, for Teacher was very beautiful and of splendid array. Her jumper was red, with golden buttons, and her collar was white, and her hair was soft, with combs. And she had a light face and a little bit of nose and teeth. Her apron was from silk with red ribbons and red flowers, and she had like man's-shoes and a watch. This vision of feminine perfection was bestowing time and smiles on him. She was actually appealing to his judgment.

"Not look like a Christian?" she was saying. "Well, then, Morris, what do I look like?"

And Morris, ever going straight to the point, replied: "You looks like a stylish Sheeny," and waited for this intoxicating praise to bring blushes to the light face he loved. It brought the blushes, but they were even redder and hotter than he had expected. There was also a gasp on which he had not counted and a queer flash in the brown eyes.

"Morris," said Teacher, "Morris, did you ever see a Sheeny with a nose like mine?"

Morris raised his head from the red jumper, climbed off the from-silk apron and solemnly contemplated the little bit of nose. The truth broke over him in sickening waves. The star of his life had set; his doll was stuffed with sawdust; his idol had feet of clay; his light-faced lady was a Christian. And yet she was his teacher and greatly to be loved, so he bore the knowledge, for her dear sake, as bravely as he could. He returned to the from-silk apron, wound a short arm round the white collar, and sobbed:

"Teacher, yiss ma'an, you'm got a Krisht nose. But don't you care, no one couldn't never to know like you ain't a for sure Sheeny the while you got such terrible Sheeny eyes. Oh, but they couldn't never to think you're a Krisht. Und say, don't you have a frightened. I wouldn't never to tell nobody. Never. I makes a swear over it. I kiss up to God. I hopes I drops down if I tells."

At the end of a month the high heels and the festive raiment appeared again, and the staff knew that the time for action had really come. They must bring the Krisht to terms before he should see Teacher in her present and irresistible array. He was always first at the trysting place, and there they would have speech with him. They arranged to escape from Room 18 before three o'clock. The Commander-in-Chief feigned a nose-bleed, the Prime Minister developed an inward agony, and the Chancellor of the Exchequer, after some moments of indecision, boldly plucked out a tottering tooth and followed - bloody but triumphant - in their wake. They found the enemy just as they had expected, and Morris, being again elected spokesman, stepped forward and took him by his dastard hand. The adversary yielded, thinking that Teacher had been forced to greater caution. The Commander-in-Chief and the Chancellor followed close behind, they having consented, in view of the enormous issues involved, to act as scouts. Around the corner they went into a dark and narrow alley, and, when they had reached a secluded spot between the high wall of the school and the blank windows of a recently burned tenement house, Morris began:

"Teacher don't wants to go on the party mit you the while she ain't got no more that kind feeling over you."

"What?" cried the astonished Doctor Ingraham.

"She don't wants to be married mit you."

"Did Miss Bailey send you with any message to me?"

The question was so fierce that the truth was forced from the unwilling lips of the spokesman.

"No ma'an - no sir," they faltered. "On'y that's the feeling what she had. Und so you go away now 'out seeing Teacher, me und the other fellows we gives you FIVE cents."

The cabinet drew near to hear the answer to this suggestion. It puzzled them, for -

"Now, look here, boy," said Doctor Ingraham, "you'd better go home and get to bed. You aren't well."

Morris conferred with his colleagues and returned with:

"We gives you SEVEN cents so you go home now 'out seeing Teacher. A nickel und two pennies so you go *now*. Und say, Miss Blake could to go by your side. She has kind feelings over you."

"Nonsense," said the man. "When will your teacher be down?"

"She ain't coming at all. She has no more feelings. So you goes now we gives you a dime and a penny. ELEVEN cents. We ain't got it; on'y we *could* to get. Teacher gives me all times pennies."

Just as the stranger was wondering how much of truth these extraordinary children knew, Teacher, calm-eyed and unruffled, appeared upon the scene. She said, as she generally did:

"Doctor Ingraham! Who would have thought to find you here!" And then, "Are you talking to my little people? They are the cleverest little things, and such friends of mine. Morris here and I are the greatest of cronies."

Teacher's manner, as she began her greeting, was serene and bright, but a gloomy, even a morose, glance from Doctor Ingraham's cold blue eye quite changed her. His voice too, considered as the voice of love, sounded sulkily as he said:

"So it seems. He has given me an answer which you refused me."

"How generous of Morris and how thoughtful! He's always trying to save me trouble. And the question, now, to which the answer belonged. May one know that?"

"You know it well enough," with a glance up and down the deserted alley, for even Patrick had realized that discretion is the better part of statesmanship.

"Oh *that*" said Teacher. "And Morris's answer?"

"No."

"They really are the cleverest children."

"Little brutes! I can't think why you come down here every day. The brats aren't in the least grateful."

"But they are. They think me perfection."

"That is the contagion of mental states."

"And they're not fond of you." "That's it again, I suppose." And, as Teacher made no sign of having heard, he went on: "Tea, do you know, is a dreadful bore."

"Of course, but cold tea is worse. And the cakes are so shattered towards the end. Come."

"I've changed my mind. I'm not going. I'm tired of this sort of thing. Answer me now."

"But the children," faltered Teacher. "I should miss them so."

At this sign of weakening Doctor Ingraham favoured the queer old street with a tableau to which it long had been a stranger. And the cabinet, creeping back to reconnoitre, immediately guessed the worst. Said Morris:

"She's lovin' mit him und he's loving mit her. They've got loving looks. I had once a auntie - "

This was too much for the torn spirit of the Leader of the Line. He laid violent hands - and feet - upon the Monitor of Gold Fish. The Monitor of Window Boxes promptly followed suit. Morris's prolonged yell of agonized surprise brought Teacher flying to the rescue. And Teacher brought Doctor Ingraham. While the latter held and restrained Patrick and Nathan, Miss Bailey lavished endearments and caresses on her favourite. The captor grew as restless as his captives under this aggravation, and at last allowed his charges to escape.

"Look here!" he remonstrated; "I can't stand this sort of thing, you know. It's cruel."

But Teacher's ears were all for Morris's tale of sorrow.

"I don't know what is mit Patrick," he was saying. "He hits me a hack somethin' fierce sooner I says about mine auntie. Und Nathan, too, is bad boys. He says you lies."

"I?" said Teacher; "I?"

"Yiss ma'an, that's how he says. On'y *I* know you don't lies. I *know* we should be monitors like you says."

"When, dearie?"

"On your weddinge. You know you says me, und Patrick, und Nathan, should be monitors on your weddinge when you marries mit him." And Morris stretched a pointing finger at the foe. After one radiant glance at Teacher's face, Doctor Ingraham possessed himself of the scrubby hand and shook it warmly.

"And so you shall, old chap," he cried, "so you shall. You may be best man if you so desire. Anything you like."

"New clothes?" asked Morris.

"From stem to stern."

"Ice-cream?"

"Gallons."

"Paper napkins mit birds?"

"Bushels."

"Can I mine little sister bring?"

"A dozen little sisters if you have them."

"Can I go in a carriage, down and up? It's stylish."

"You shall have a parade of carriages - one for each sister."

"Morris," commanded Miss Bailey, "go home."

When she turned to confront Doctor Ingraham the "light face" was brightly pink and the "terrible Sheeny eyes" held a mixture of embarrassment and anger.

"Of course I can't explain this," she said. "I must simply ask you to believe that he is making a dreadful mistake. You were quite right when you said they were ungrateful little brutes. They are. You were quite right, too, about teas being a bore. They are. So you will pardon me if I go to see little Leah Yonowsky. The twins are reported ill again. Good afternoon."

It was a very rueful and disgusted enemy that the cabinet discerned in the offing.

"Good Lord!" cried the Commander-in-Chief. "Here he comes again, and Miss Bailey ain't with him."

"Morris," said the enemy, "you've done for me, my boy."

"Won't she go by your side on the party?" asked the Prime Minister.

"She will not," admitted the hostile power. "So you may as well trot out Miss Blake and begin to collect my eleven cents. For, though you may not have discovered it - and there be those who doubt it - a ten-cent cigar's a smoke."

MORRIS AND THE HONOURABLE TIM

On the first day of school, after the Christmas holidays, Teacher found herself surrounded by a howling mob of little savages in which she had much difficulty in recognizing her cherished First-Reader Class. Isidore Belchatosky's face was so wreathed in smiles and foreign matter as to be beyond identification; Nathan Spiderwitz had placed all his trust in a solitary suspender and two unstable buttons; Eva Kidansky had entirely freed herself from restraining hooks and eyes; Isidore Applebaum had discarded shoe-laces; and Abie Ashnewsky had bartered his only necktie for a yard of "shoe-string" licorice.

Miss Bailey was greatly disheartened by this reversion to the original type. She delivered daily lectures on nail-brushes, hair-ribbons, shoe polish, pins, buttons, elastic, and other means to grace. Her talks on soap and water became almost personal in tone, and her insistence on a close union between such garments as were meant to be united, led to a lively traffic in twisted and disreputable safety-pins. And yet the First-Reader Class, in all other branches of learning so receptive and responsive, made but halting and uncertain progress towards thatstate of virtue which is next to godliness.

Early in January came the report that "Gum Shoe Tim"

was on the war-path and might be expected at any time. Miss Bailey heard the tidings in calm ignorance until Miss Blake, who ruled over the adjoining kingdom, interpreted the warning. A license to teach in the public schools of New York is good for only one year. Its renewal depends upon the reports of the Principal in charge of the school and of the Associate Superintendent in whose district the school chances to be. After three such renewals the license becomes permanent, but Miss Bailey was, as a teacher, barely four months old. The Associate Superintendent for her vicinity was the Honourable Timothy O'Shea, known and dreaded as "Gum Shoe Tim," owing to his engaging way of creeping softly up back stairs and appearing, all unheralded and unwelcome, upon the threshold of his intended victim.

This, Miss Blake explained, was in defiance of all the rules of etiquette governing such visits of inspection. The proper procedure had been that of Mr. O'Shea's predecessor, who had always given timely notice of his coming and a hint as to the subjects in which he intended to examine the children. Some days later he would amble from room to room, accompanied by the amiable Principal, and followed by the gratitude of smiling and unruffled teachers.

This kind old gentleman was now retired and had been succeeded by Mr. O'Shea, who, in addition to his unexpectedness, was adorned by an abominable temper, an overbearing manner, and a sense of cruel humour. He had almost finished his examinations at the nearest school where, during a brisk campaign of eight days, he had caused five dismissals, nine cases of nervous exhaustion, and an epidemic of hysteria.

Day by day nerves grew more tense, tempers more unsure, sleep and appetite more fugitive. Experienced teachers went stolidly on with the ordinary routine while beginners devoted time and energy to the more spectacular portions of the curriculum. But no one knew the Honourable Timothy's pet subjects and so no one could specialize to any great extent.

Miss Bailey was one of the beginners, and Room 18 was made to shine as the sun. Morris Mogilewsky, Monitor of the Gold-Fish Bowl, wrought busily until his charges glowed redly against the water plants in their shining bowl. Creepers crept, plants grew, and ferns waved under the care of Nathan Spiderwitz, Monitor of the Window Boxes. There was such a martial swing and strut in Patrick Brennan's leadership of the line that it informed even the timid heart of Isidore Wishnewsky with a war-like glow and his feet with a spasmodic but well-meant tramp. Sadie Gonorowsky and Eva, her cousin, sat closely side by side, no longer "mad on theirselves," but "mit kind feelings." The work of the preceding term was laid in neat and docketed piles upon the low book-case. The children were enjoined to keep clean and entire. And Teacher, a nervous and unsmiling Teacher, waited dully.

A week passed thus, and then the good-hearted and experienced Miss Blake hurried ponderously across the hall to put Teacher on her guard.

"I've just had a note from one of the grammar teachers," she panted. "'Gum Shoe Tim' is up in Miss Greene's room. He'll take this floor next. Now, see here, child, don't look so frightened. The Principle is with Tim. Of course you're nervous, but try not to show it. And you'll be all right, his lay is discipline and reading. Well, good luck to you!"

Miss Bailey took heart of grace. The children read surprisingly well, were absolutely good, and the enemy under convoy of the friendly Principal would be much less terrifying than the enemy at large and alone. It was, therefore, with a manner almost serene that she turned to greet the kindly concerned Principal and the dreaded "Gum Shoe Tim." The latter she found less ominous of aspect than she had been led to fear, and the Principal's charming little speech of introduction made her flush with quick pleasure. And the anxious eyes of Sadie Gonorowsky, noting the flush, grew calm as Sadie whispered to Eva, her close cousin:

"Say, Teacher has a glad. She's red on the face. It could to be her papa."

"No. It's comp'ny," answered Eva sagely. "It ain't her papa. It's comp'ny the whiles Teacher takes him by the hand."

The children were not in the least disconcerted by the presence of the large man. They always enjoyed visitors and they liked the heavy gold chain which festooned the wide white waistcoat of this guest; and, asthey watched him, the Associate Superintendent began to superintend.

He looked at the children all in their clean and smiling rows: he looked at the flowers and the gold fish; at the pictures and the plaster casts: he looked at the work of the last term and he looked at Teacher. As he looked he swayed gently on his rubber heels and decided that he was going to enjoy the coming quarter of an hour.

Teacher pleased him from the first. She was neither old nor ill-favoured, and she was most evidently nervous. The combination appealed both to his love of power and his peculiar sense of humour. Settling deliberately in the chair of state, he began:

"Can the children sing, Miss Bailey?"

They could sing very prettily and they did.

"Very nice, indeed," said the voice of visiting authority. "Very nice. Their music is exceptionally good. And are they drilled? Children, will you march for me?"

Again they could and did. Patrick marshaled his line in time and triumph up and down the aisles to the evident interest and approval of the "comp'ny," and then Teacher led the class through some very energetic Swedish movements. While arms and bodies were bending and straightening at Teacher's command and example, the door opened and a breathless boy rushed in. He bore an unfolded note and, as Teacher had no hand to spare, the boy placed the paper on the desk under the softening eyes of the Honourable Timothy, who glanced down idly and then pounced upon the note and read its every word.

"For you, Miss Bailey," he said in the voice before which even the school janitor had been known to quail. "Your friend was thoughtful, though a little late." And poor palpitating Miss Bailey read.

"Watch out! 'Gum Shoe Tim' is in the building. The Principal caught him on the back stairs and they're going round together. He's as cross as a bear. Greene in dead faint in dressing-room. Says he's going to fire her. Watch out for him, and send the news on. His lay is reading and discipline."

Miss Bailey grew cold with sick and unreasoning fear. As she gazed wide-eyed at the living confirmation of the statement that "Gum Shoe Tim" was "as cross as a bear," the gentle-hearted Principal took the paper from her nerveless grasp.

"It's all right," he assured her. "Mr. O'Shea understands that you had no part in this. It's *all* right. You are not responsible."

But Teacher had no ears for his soothing. She could only watch with fascinated eyes as the Honourable Timothy reclaimed the note and wrote across it's damning face: "Miss Greene may come to. She is not fired. - T.O'S."

"Here, boy," he called; "take this to your teacher." The puzzled messenger turned to obey, and the Associate Superintendent saw that though his dignity had suffered his power had increased. To the list of those whom he might, if so disposed, devour, he had now added the name of the Principal, who was quick to understand that an unpleasant investigation lay before him. If Miss Bailey could not be held responsible for this system of inter-classroom communication, it was clear that the Principal could.

Every trace of interest had left Mr. O'Shea's voice as he asked:

"Can they read?"

"Oh, yes, they read," responded Teacher, but her spirit was crushed and the children reflected her depression. Still, they were marvellously good and that blundering note had said, "Discipline is his lay." Well, here he had it.

There was one spectator of this drama, who, understanding no word nor incident therein, yet missed no shade of the many emotions which had stirred the light face of his lady. Towards the front of the room sat Morris Mogilewsky, with every nerve tuned to Teacher's, and with an appreciation of the situation in which the other children had no share. On the afternoon of one of those dreary days of waiting for the evil which had now come, Teacher had endeavoured to explain the nature and possible result of this ordeal to her favourite. It was clear to him now that she was troubled, and he held the large and unaccustomed presence of the comp'ny mit whiskers responsible. Countless generations of ancestors had followed and fostered the instinct which now led Morris to propitiate an angry power. Luckily, he was prepared with an offering of a suitable nature. He had meant to enjoy it for yet a few days, and then to give it to Teacher. She was such a sensible person about presents. One might give her one's most cherished possession with a brave and cordial heart, for on each Friday afternoon she returned the gifts she had received during the week. And this with no abatement of gratitude.

Morris rose stealthily, crept forward, and placed a bright blue bromo-seltzer bottle in the fat hand which hung over the back of the chair of state. The hand closed instinctively as, with dawning curiosity, the Honourable Timothy studied the small figure at his side. It began in a wealth of loosely curling hair which shaded a delicate face, very pointed as to chin and monopolized by a pair of dark eyes, sad and deep and beautiful. A faded blue "jumper" was buttoned tightly across the narrow chest; frayed trousers were precariously attached to the "jumper," and impossible shoes and stockings supplemented the trousers. Glancing from boy to bottle, the "comp'ny mit whiskers" asked:

"What's this for?"

"For you."

"What's in it?"

"A present."

Mr. O'Shea removed the cork and proceeded to draw out incredible quantities of absorbent cotton. When there was no more to come, a faint tinkle sounded within the blue depths, and Mr. O'Shea, reversing the bottle, found himself possessed of a trampled and disfigured sleeve link of most palpable brass.

"It's from gold," Morris assured him. "You puts it in your - 'scuse me - shirt. Wish you health to wear it."

"Thank you," said the Honourable Tim, and there was a tiny break in the gloom which had enveloped him. And then, with a quick memory of the note and of his anger:

"Miss Bailey, who is this young man?"

And Teacher, of whose hobbies Morris was one, answered warmly: "That is Morris Mogilewsky, the best of boys. He takes care of the gold-fish, and does all sorts of things for me. Don't you, dear?"

"Teacher, yiss ma'an," Morris answered.

"I'm lovin' much mit you. I gives presents on the company over you."

"Aint he rather big to speak such broken English?" asked Mr. O'Shea. "I hope you remember that it is part of your duty to stamp out the dialect."

"Yes, I know," Miss Bailey answered. "But Morris has been in America for so short a time. Nine months, is it not?"

"Teacher, yiss ma'an. I comes out of Russia," responded Morris, on the verge of tears and with his face buried in Teacher's dress.

Now Mr. O'Shea had his prejudices - strong and deep. He had been given jurisdiction over that particular district because it was his native heath, and the Board of Education considered that he would be more in sympathy with the inhabitants than a stranger. The truth was absolutely the reverse. Because he had spent his early years in a large old house on East Broadway, because he now saw his birthplace changed to a squalid tenement, and the happy hunting grounds of his youth grown ragged and foreign - swarming with strange faces and noisy with strange tongues - Mr. O'Shea bore a sullen grudge against the usurping race.

He resented the caressing air with which Teacher held the little hand placed so confidently within her own and he welcomed the opportunity of gratifying his still ruffled temper and his racial antagonism at the same time. He would take a rise out of this young woman about her little Jew. She would be comforted later on. Mr. O'Shea rather fancied himself in the role of comforter, when the sufferer was neither old nor ill-favoured. And so he set about creating the distress which he would later change to gratitude and joy. Assuredly the Honourable Timothy had a well-developed sense of humour.

"His English is certainly dreadful," remarked the voice of authority, and it was not an English voice, nor is O'Shea distinctively an English name. "Dreadful. And, by the way, I hope you are not spoiling these youngsters. You must remember that you are fitting them for the battle of life. Don't coddle your soldiers. Can you reconcile your present attitude with discipline?"

"With Morris - yes," Teacher answered. "He is gentle and tractable beyond words."

"Well, I hope you're right," grunted Mr. O'Shea "but don't coddle them."

And so the incident closed. The sleeve link was tucked, before Morris's yearning eyes, into the reluctant pocket of the wide white waistcoat, and Morris returned to his place. He found his reader and the proper page, and the lesson went on with brisk serenity: real on the children's part, but bravely assumed on Teacher's. Child after child stood up; read; sat down again; and it came to be the duty of Bertha Binderwitz to read the entire page of which the others had each read a line. She began jubilantly, but soon stumbled, hesitated, and wailed: "Stands a fierce word. I don't know what it is," and Teacher turned to write the puzzling word upon the blackboard.

Morris's heart stopped with a sickening suddenness and then rushed madly on again. He had a new and dreadful duty to perform. All his mother's counsel, all his father's precepts told him that it was his duty. Yet fear held him in his little seat behind his little desk, while his conscience insisted on this unalterable decree of the social code: "So somebody's clothes is wrong it's polite you says 'scuse' und tells it out."

And here was Teacher whom he dearly loved, whose ideals of personal adornment extended to full sets of buttons on jumpers and to laces in both shoes, here was his immaculate lady fair in urgent need of assistance and advice, and all because she had on that day inaugurated a delightfully vigorous exercise for which, architecturally, she was not designed.

There was yet room for hope that some one else would see the breach and brave the danger. But no. The visitor sat stolidly in the chair of state, the Principal sat serenely beside him, the children sat each in his own little place, behind his own little desk, keeping his own little eyes on his own little book. No. Morris's soul cried with Hamlet's:

> "*The time is out of joint; - O cursed spite,*
> *That ever I was born to set it right!*"

Up into the quiet air went his timid hand. Teacher, knowing him in his more garrulous moods, ignored the threatened interruption of Bertha's spirited resume, but the windmill action of the little arm attracted the Honourable Tim's attention.

"The best of boys wants you," he suggested, and Teacher perforce asked:

"Well, Morris, what is it?"

Not until he was on his feet did the Monitor of the Gold-Fish Bowl, appreciate the enormity of the mission he had undertaken. The other children began to understand, and watched his struggle for words and breath with sympathy or derision, as their natures prompted. But there are no words in which one may politely mention ineffective safety-pins to one's glass of fashion. Morris's knees trembled queerly, his breathing grew difficult, and Teacher seemed a very great way off as she asked again:

"Well, what is it, dear?"

Morris panted a little, smiled weakly, and then sat down. Teacher was evidently puzzled, the "Comp'ny" alert, the Principal uneasy.

"Now, Morris," Teacher remonstrated, "you must tell me what you want."

But Morris had deserted his etiquette and his veracity, and murmured only:

"Nothings."

"Just wanted to be noticed," said the Honourable Tim. "It is easy to spoil them." And he watched the best of boys rather closely, for a habit of interrupting reading lessons, wantonly and without reason, was a trait in the young of which he disapproved.

When this disapprobation manifested itself in Mr. O'Shea's countenance, the loyal heart of Morris interpreted it as a new menace to his sovereign. No later than yesterday she had warned them of the vital importance of coherence. "Every one knows," she had said, "that only common little boys and girls come apart. No one ever likes them," and the big stranger was even now misjudging her.

Again his short arm agitated the quiet air. Again his trembling legs upheld a trembling boy. Again authority urged. Again Teacher asked:

"Well, Morris, what is it, dear?"

All this was as before, but not as before was poor harassed Miss Bailey's swoop down the aisle, her sudden taking of Morris's troubled little face between her soft hands, the quick near meeting with her kind eyes, the note of pleading in her repetition:

"What do you want, Morris?"

He was beginning to answer when it occurred to him that the truth might make her cry. There was an unsteadiness about her upper lip which seemed to indicate the possibility. Suddenly he found that he no longer yearned for words in which to tell her of her disjointment, but for something else - anything else - to say.

His miserable eyes escaped from hers and wandered to the wall in desperate search for conversation. There was no help in the pictures, no inspiration in the plaster casts, but on the blackboard he read, "Tuesday, January twenty-first, 1902." Only the date, but he must make it serve. With Teacher close beside him, with the hostile eye of the Honourable Tim upon him, hedged round about by the frightened or admiring regard of the First-Reader Class, Morris blinked rapidly, swallowed resolutely, and remarked:

"Teacher, this year's Nineteen-hundred-and-two," and knew that all was over.

The caressing clasp of Teacher's hands grew into a grip of anger. The countenance of Mr. O'Shea took on the beatified expression of the prophet who has found honour and verification in his own country.

"The best of boys has his off days and this is one of them," he remarked.

"Morris," said Teacher, "did you stop a reading lesson to tell me that? Do you think I don't know what the year is? I'm ashamed of you."

Never had she spoken thus. If the telling had been difficult to Morris when she was "glad on him," it was impossible now that she was a prey to such evident "mad feelings." And yet he must make some explanation. So he murmured: "Teacher, I tells you 'scuse. I know you knows what year stands, on'y it's polite I tells you something, und I had a fraid."

"And so you bothered your Teacher with that nonsense," said Tim. "You're a nice boy!"

Morris's eyes were hardly more appealing than Teacher's as the two culprits, for so they felt themselves, turned to their judge.

"Morris is a strange boy," Miss Bailey explained. "He can't be managed by ordinary methods - "

"And extraordinary methods don't seem to work today," Mr. O'Shea interjected.

" - and I think," Teacher continued, "that it might be better not to press the point."

"Oh, if you have no control over him - " Mr. O'Shea was beginning pleasantly, when the Principal suggested:

"You'd better let us hear what he has to say, Miss Bailey; make him understand that you are master here." And Teacher, with a heart-sick laugh at the irony of this advice in the presence of the Associate Superintendent, turned to obey.

But Morris would utter no words but these, dozens of times repeated: "I have a fraid." Miss Bailey coaxed, bribed, threatened and cajoled; shook him surreptitiously, petted him openly. The result was always the same: "It's polite I tells you something out, on'y I had a fraid."

"But, Morris, dear, of what?" cried Teacher. "Are you afraid of me? Stop crying now and answer. Are you afraid of Miss Bailey?"

"N-o-o-oh m-a-a-an."

"Are you afraid of the Principal?"

"N-o-o-oh m-a-a-an."

"Are you afraid" - with a slight pause, during which a native hue of honesty was foully done to death - "of the kind gentleman we are all so glad to see?"

"N-o-o-oh m-a-a-an."

"Well, then, what is the matter with you? Are you sick? Don't you think you would like to go home to your mother?"

"N-o-o-oh m-a-a-an; I ain't sick. I tells you 'scuse."

The repeated imitation of a sorrowful goat was too much for the Honourable Tim.

"Bring that boy to me," he commanded. "I'll show you how to manage refractory and rebellious children."

With much difficulty and many assurances that the gentleman was not going to hurt him, Miss Bailey succeeded in untwining Morris's legs from the supports of the desk and in half carrying, half leading him up to the chair of state. An ominous silence had settled over the room. Eva Gonorowsky was weeping softly, and the redoubtable Isidore Applebaum was stiffened in a frozen calm.

"Morris," began the Associate Superintendent in his most awful tones, "will you tell me why you raised your hand? Come here, sir." Teacher urged him gently, and like dog to heel, he went. He halted within a pace or two of Mr. O'Shea, and lifted a beseeching face towards him.

"I couldn't to tell nothing out," said he. "I tells you 'scuse. I'm got a fraid."

The Honourable Tim lunged quickly and caught the terrified boy preparatory to shaking him, but Morris escaped and fled to his haven of safety - his Teacher's arms. When Miss Bailey felt the quick clasp of the thin little hands, the heavy beating of the over-tried heart, and the deep convulsive sobs, she turned on the Honourable Timothy O'Shea and spoke:

"I must ask you to leave this room at once," she announced. The Principal started, and then sat back. Teacher's eyes were dangerous, and the Honourable Tim might profit by a lesson. "You've frightened the child until he can't breathe. I can do nothing with him while you remain. The examination is ended. You may go."

Now Mr. O'Shea saw he had gone a little too far in his effort to create the proper dramatic setting for his clemency. He had not expected the young woman to "rise" quite so far and high. His deprecating half-apology, half-eulogy, gave Morris the opportunity he craved.

"Teacher." he panted; "I wants to whisper mit you in the ear."

With a dexterous movement he knelt upon her lap and tore out his solitary safety-pin. He then clasped her tightly and made his explanation. He began in the softest of whispers, which increased in volume as it did in interest, so that he reached the climax at the full power of his boy soprano voice.

"Teacher, Missis Bailey, I know you know what year stands. On'y it's polite I tells you something, und I had a fraid the while the comp'ny mit the whiskers sets und rubbers. But, Teacher, it's like this: your jumper's sticking out und you could to take mine safety-pin."

He had understood so little of all that had passed that he was beyond being surprised by the result of this communication. Miss Bailey had gathered him into her arms and had cried in a queer helpless way. And as she cried she had said over and over again: "Morris, how could you? Oh, how could you, dear? How *could* you?"

The Principal and "the comp'ny mit whiskers" had looked solemnly at one another for a struggling moment, and had then broken into laughter, long and loud, until the visiting authority was limp and moist. The children waited in polite uncertainty, but when Miss Bailey, after some indecision, had contributed a wan smile, which later grew into a shaky laugh, the First-Reader Class went wild.

Then the Honourable Timothy arose to say good-by. He reiterated his praise of the singing and reading, the blackboard work and the moral tone. An awkward pause ensued, during which the Principal engaged the young Gonorowskys in impromptu conversation. The Honourable Tim crossed over to Miss Bailey's side and steadied himself for a great effort.

"Teacher," he began meekly, "I tells you 'scuse. This sort of thing makes a man feel like a bull in a china shop. Do you think the little fellow will shake hands with me? I was really only joking."

"But surely he will," said Miss Bailey, as she glanced down at the tangle of dark curls resting against her breast. "Morris, dear, aren't you going to say good-by to the gentleman?"

Morris relaxed one hand from its grasp on his lady and bestowed it on Mr. O'Shea.

"Good by," said he gently. "I gives you presents, from gold presents, the while you're friends mit Teacher. I'm loving much mit her too."

At this moment the Principal turned, and Mr. O'Shea, in a desperate attempt to retrieve his dignity, began: "As to class management and discipline - "

But the Principal was not to be deceived.

"Don't you think, Mr. O'Shea," said he, "that you and I had better leave the management of the little ones to the women? You have noticed, perhaps, that this is Nature's method."

WHEN A MAN'S WIDOWED

It was a quarter past nine and Miss Bailey was calling the roll, an undertaking which, after months of daily practice, was still formidable. Beginning with Abraham Abrahamowsky and continuing through the alphabet to Solomon Zaracheck, the roll-call of the First-Reader Class was full of stumbling blocks and pitfalls. Teacher insisted upon absolute silence during the five minutes thus consumed, and so it chanced that the excitement of Miss Blake, bursting into Room 18 at this particular time, was thrown into strong relief against the prevailing peace.

"Miss Bailey," began the ruffled sovereign of the room across the hall, "did the Principal speak to you about one of my boys being put back into your grade?"

"Oh, yes; some weeks ago."

"Well, he has been absent ever since, but he turned up this morning. Are you ready to take him now?"

"But of course - How old is he?"

"Nearly seven. Too old for your grade and too advanced, but the Principal wants you to have him because my boys laugh at him. His mother is dead, his sisters in an orphan asylum, and we thought that your little girls might have a civilizing influence over him."

"Perhaps they may," Teacher cheerfully acquiesced. "Eva Gonorowsky alone would civilize a whole tribe of savages. Will you bring him to me?"

The door of Room 17 was not quite closed, and from behind it came sounds of talking and of laughter. Miss Blake threw a few words upon the turmoil, and silence immediately ensued. Then said she: "Isidore Diamantstein, come here," and the only result was a slight titter.

"Abie Fishhandler," she next commanded, "bring Diamantstein to Miss Bailey's room."

The tittering increased and to it were added a scuffle and a sleepily fretful "Lemme be." A heavy footstep crossed the hall and the stalwart Abie Fishhandler stalked into Room 18, bearing the new boy in his arms. From his dusty unlaced shoes to his jungle of gleaming red hair, Isidore Diamantstein was inert, dirty, and bedraggled.

"Oh, let him stand!" cried Miss Blake sharply. "Here, Diamantstein, what's the matter with you? This is Miss Bailey, your new teacher."

"How do you do, Isidore?" said Miss Bailey, as she stooped and took his hand. Then she added quickly to Miss Blake: "He seems feverish. Is he ill?" "Perhaps he is," the other answered. "I never saw him so queer as he is this morning. You'd better let the doctor see him when he comes."

But long before the eleven o'clock visit of the

physician of the Board of Health, the illness of Isidore had reached its crisis. When Miss Bailey had established him in his new place he had seen nothing of his surroundings and had been quite deaf to the greetings, whether shy or jeering, with which the First-Reader Class had welcomed him. Left to his own devices, he had promptly laid his arms upon his desk and his head upon his arms. Five minutes passed. Ten minutes. Isidore's brilliant head still rested on his folded arms and Teacher felt that she must make some effort to comfort his wordless misery.

"Isidore," she began, bending over him, "you won't have to stay here very long. You may go back to Miss Blake in a few days if you are good. So now, dear boy, cheer up!" But as she patted the shoulder nearest to her a long sigh quivered through the little body.

"Now, don't do that," Miss Bailey urged. "Isidore, sit up nicely and let me look at you," and, slipping her hand beneath the chin, she turned the face up to hers. She was prepared for tear-drenched eyes and trembling lips but she found neither. Isidore's dark-lashed lids drooped heavily over his unseeing eyes, his head rolled loosely from side to side, and he began to slip, silently and unconsciously to the floor.

Teacher, in wild alarm, bore him to an open window and sent Patrick Brennan in flying search of the Principal. A great revulsion shook her whenever she looked at the blank little face, but she never guessed the truth. Patrick's quest was short and the Principal's first glance sufficient.

"Send for the janitor," he commanded, and then, "Miss Bailey, may I speak to you in the hall?"

Myra Kelly

Teacher invested Morris Mogilewsky in the chair and the position of authority, sent Patrick for the janitor, and, strangely shaken, followed the Principal.

"What is it?" she asked, miserably, when the door was closed. "What is the matter with that baby?"

"Well," said the Principal kindly, "if you were more experienced you would be less shocked than I fear you are going to be. The child is simply and most abominably drunk."

"Drunk!" gasped Miss Bailey. "Drunk! and not seven years old!"

"Drunk," echoed the Principal. "Poor little chap! Did Miss Blake tell you the history? - The mother dead, the father away all day, no woman's care. Of course, the end will be the reformatory, but I wonder if we can do anything before that end is reached?"

"Oh, it can't be quite hopeless!" cried Miss Bailey. "Please give him to me. But I want to see that father."

"So you shall," the Principal assured her. "I shall send for him to-morrow to explain this. But he will be entirely at sea. I have him here every two or three weeks about one or other of his children - there are two boys in the upper grades - and the poor devil never can explain. However, I shall let you know when he is here."

The morrow proved the Principal's surmise to have been correct. Mr. Lazarus Diamantstein stood in helpless and hopeless misery before a court of inquiry comprising the Principal, Miss Bailey, the physician of the Board of Health, a representative of the Gerry Society, the truant officer, the indignant janitor, and a policeman who had come to the school in reference to the florid language of his own small son, and, for scenic effect, was pressed into service. Mr. Diamantstein turned from one to another of these stern-faced officials and to each in turn he made his unaltered plea:

"Mine leetle Izzie was a goot leetle boy. He don't never make like you says. Ach! never, never!"

Again, for effect, scenic or moral, the Principal indicated one of the hostile figures of the court. "This gentleman," said he, "belongs to a society which will take charge of your son. Have you ever, Mr. Diamantstein, heard of the Gerry Society?"

Poor Mr. Diamantstein cowered. In all the terrifying world in which he groped so darkly, the two forces against which he had been most often warned were the Board of Health, which might at any time and without notice wash out one's house and confiscate one's provisions; and the Gerry Society, which washed one's children with soap made from the grease of pigs, and fed them with all sorts of "traef" and unblessed meat.

"Ach, no!" he implored. "Gott, no! You should not take and make so mit mine' leetle boy. He ain't a bad boy. He sure ain't."

"Really, I don't think he is," Miss Bailey's cool and quiet voice interposed, and in a moment the harassed father was at her side pleading, extenuating, fawning.

"That young lady," said the Principal, "is your only

hope. If Miss Bailey - " Mr. Diamantstein interpreted this as an introduction and bowed most wonderfully - "If Miss Bailey will keep Isidore in her class he may stay in the school. If not, this gentleman - By the way, Miss Bailey, is he at school to-day?"

"Oh, yes, and behaving beautifully. Perhaps his father would care to see him. Will you come with me, Mr. Diamantstein?"

Yearnings to see the cause of all this trouble and sorrow were not very strong in the paternal bosom, but Mr. Diamantstein welcomed the opportunity to escape from officialdom and inquiry.

As she led the way to Room 18, Teacher was again impressed by the furtive helplessness of the man. Living in a land whose language was well-nigh unintelligible to him, ruled and judged by laws whose existence he could learn only by breaking them, driven out of one country, unwelcomed in another, Mr. Diamantstein was indeed a wanderer and an outcast. Some note of sympathy found its way into Miss Bailey's efforts at conversation, and Mr. Diamantstein's quick ear detected it. The vision of Isidore in his new surroundings, the pictures and flowers, the swinging canary and the plaster casts, impressed him mightily, while Miss Bailey's evident and sincere interest in his efforts to do what he could for his boys took him entirely by surprise. He admonished Isidore to super-human efforts towards the reformation which might keep him in this beautiful room and under the care of its lady, and, as he was about to return to his neglected sewing machine, he gave Miss Bailey all he had to give:

"Say, Teacher," said he, with a wistful glance at his frail little son; "say, you want to lick Issie? Well, you can."

"Oh, thank you very much, Mr. Diamantstein" returned Miss Bailey, while Isidore, thus bestowed, wept aloud, and required instant soothing. "That's very good of you, but I hope it won't be necessary."

"Well," said the father generously, "so you *want* lick, so you *can* lick." And so departed.

Miss Bailey's new responsibility continued to behave beautifully. He was peacefully disposed towards the other boys, who feared and venerated him as a member of the "Clinton Street gang." He fell promptly captive to the dark and gentle charms of Eva Gonorowsky and to the calm dominion of Teacher. To the latter he showed a loving confidence which she met with a broad-minded tolerance, very wonderful to his eyes in a person of authority. She seemed really to understand the sweet reasonableness of the reminiscences with which he entertained her. And if she sometimes deplored the necessity of so much lying, stealing, fighting and late hours, well so, of late, did he. She asked him quite calmly one day what he had had for breakfast on the morning of his first day in Room 18, and how he had chanced to be so drunk, and he, with true economy, answered two questions with one word:

"Beer."

"And where," asked Teacher, still carefully unimpressed "did you get it? From your father?"

"Naw," said Isidore, whose manners were yet

unformed "He don't never get no beer. He ain't got a can even."

"Then where?"

"To the s'loon - "

"And which saloon?" Miss Bailey's quiet eyes betrayed no trace of her determination that the proprietor should suffer the full penalty of the law. "I thought little boys were not allowed into saloons."

"Well," Isidore admitted, "I ain't gone in the s'loon. I tells the lady on our floor that my papa likes that she should lend her can und she says, 'He's welcome, all right.' Und I gives the can on a man what stands by the s'loon, und I says: 'My papa he has a sickness, und beer is healthy for him. On'y he couldn't to come for buy none. You could to take a drink for yourself.' Und the man says, 'Sure.' Und he gets the beer und takes the drink - a *awful* big drink - und I sets by the curb und drinks what is in the can. It's awful nice for me."

Miss Bailey's hope for any real or lasting moral change in Isidore was sadly shaken by this revelation. Six and a half years old and deliberately plotting and really enjoying a drunken debauch! Surely, the reformatory seemed inevitable. Suddenly she became conscious that the chain of circumstance in Isidore's recital was not complete.

"But the money," she asked; "where did you get that?"

Isidore's eyes were wells of candour as he answered: "Off a lady."

"And why did she give it to you?"

"'Cause I tells her my mamma lays on the hospital und I like I should buy her a orange on'y I ain't got no money for buy none."

"Oh, Isidore!" cried Teacher, in a voice in which horror, pity, reproach, and wonder mingled. "And you have no mother!" And Isidore's answer was his professional whine, most heartrending and insincere.

Gradually and carefully Teacher became slightly censorious and mildly didactic, and slowly Isidore Diamantstein came to forsake the paths of evil and to spend long afternoons in the serene and admiring companionship of Morris Mogilewsky, Patrick Brennan and Nathan Spiderwitz. But when, early in December, he found a stranded comic valentine and presented it, blushingly, to Eva Gonorowsky, Miss Bailey found that success was indeed most sweet.

Mr. Diamantstein's visits to the school, directed with patient futility to the propitiation of the teachers of his older sons, always ended in a cheering little talk with the young ruler of Room 18. To her he confided his history, his difficulties, and his hopes. In return she gave him advice, encouragement, and, in moments of too pressing need, assistance. The need of this kind was, however, rare, for Mr. Diamantstein was an expert in one of the most difficult branches of the tailor's art, and his salary better than that of many of his fellows.

Shortly after the incident of the valentine Mr. Diamantstein came to Room 18 in radiant array. His frock coat was new and of a wondrous fashion, his tan shoes were of superlative length and sharpness of toe, both his coat and vest were open to the lowest button and turned back to give due prominence to the bright blue shirt beneath. His hair shone in luxurious and oiled profusion, and in the collarless band of his shirt, a chaste diamond stud, not much larger than a butter-plate, flashed and shimmered through his curled black beard. It was luncheon lime, and Teacher was at liberty.

"Say, Missis Pailey," he began, "what you think? I'm a loafer."

"Did you give up your position?" asked Miss Bailey, "or did you lose it? You can easily get another, I hope."

"You not understand," cried the guest eagerly. "I was one great big loafer," and he laid outstretched hands upon the blue bosom of his gala shirt; "one great big loafer man."

"No, I'm afraid I don't understand," confessed Miss Bailey. "Tell me about it."

"Vell, I was a vidder man," Mr. Diamantstein explained. "Mine vife she die. From long she die, und I'm a vidder man. But now I marry, maybe, again. I ain't no more a vidder man. I was a loafer on a beautiful yonge lady."

"Oh! you're a lover, Mr. Diamantstein. Why, that's the best news I've heard for ages! And your new wife will take care of the boys. I am so glad!"

"She's a beautiful yonge lady," the Lothario continued;

"but easy scared! Oh, awful easy scared! So I don't tell her nothings over those devil boys."

"Now, Mr. Diamantstein - " Teacher began admonishingly, but he interrupted.

"I tells her like this: 'Say, ain't it nice? I got three leetle poys - awful nice leetle poys - no one ain't never seen no better leetle poys.' Und she says she won't marry mit me. Ain't I tell you how she's easy scared? But I tells her all times how my leetle poys is goot, how they makes for her the work, und the dinner, und the beds. Und now she says she will marry mit me und I'm a loafer on a beautiful yonge uptown lady."

The wild gesticulations of Mr. Diamantstein during this account of his courtship and of its triumphant conclusion were wonderful to see. He stopped now, glowing and panting, and Teacher noticed, for the first time, that he was still a young man, and that there was some shadow of excuse for the reckless course of the "beautiful yonge uptown lady."

"Mr. Diamantstein," she said heartily, "I wish you joy. I'm sure you deserve it, and I hope the young lady will be as good as she is beautiful. Bring her to see me some day, won't you?"

"Sure," said Mr. Diamantstein politely.

But ah, for the plans of mice and men! and oh, for the slip and the lip! Within that very week the airy castle of Mr. Diamantstein's hopes was shaken to its foundations. The cause was, of course, "them devil poys." Julius and Nathan Diamantstein were convicted of having stolen and offered for sale books, pencils, and paper, the property of the Board of Education. Isidore had acted as agent and was condemned as an accomplice. The father was sent for and the trio were expelled.

Then deep was the grief of Miss Bailey, and wild was the wailing of Mr. Diamantstein. He tore his hair, he clung to the hem of Miss Bailey's garment and he noted incidentally that it was of "all from wool goods," he cast his cherished derby upon the floor and himself upon her protection.

"Say, Missis Pailey," he implored, "you do me the favour? You go on the Brincipal und you say like that: 'I give him five dollars, maybe, so he don't egspell them devil poys.'"

"But he must," Teacher answered sadly. "It is the law. They must be expelled. But oh, Mr. Diamantstein, won't you try to take care of Isidore?"

"Say, Missis Pailey," Mr. Diamantstein recommenced, "you do me the favour? You go on the Brincipal und you say like that: 'I give him five dollars, maybe, so he don't egspell the boys till the month.' It makes mit me then nothings."

"You won't mind at the end of the month?" exclaimed Miss Bailey. "Why not?"

"Well," said the lover tenderly, "it's over that beautiful yonge lady. She's awful easy scared! awful easy! Und sooner she knows them boys is egspell she don't marry no more mit me. On'y by the month she will be married already und nothings makes then nothings. Say, I gives you too, maybe, a nice present so you says like that on the Brincipal."

But Mr. Diamantstein's lavish promises could avail nothing and the boys were doomed. Time passed and Isidore's place in Miss Bailey's kingdom was taken by another American citizen in the making, and the incident seemed closed.

On an afternoon in the first week of February, Miss Bailey, Nathan Spiderwitz, and Morris Mogilewsky were busily putting Room 18 to rights, when a small boy, in an elaborate sailor costume, appeared before them. He was spotlessly clean and the handkerchief in the pocket of his blouse was dazzling in its white abundance. Upon his brow, soap-polished until it shone, there lay two smooth and sticky curves of auburn hair, and on his face there played a smile of happy recognition and repressed pride.

Miss Bailey and her ministers stood at gaze until the new comer, with a glad cry of "Teacher, oh, mine Teacher," threw himself upon the lady, and then surprise gave place to joy.

"Isidore, my dear boy; I'm so glad to see you! And how beautiful you look!" cried Teacher.

"Beautiful and stylish," said Morris generously. "Sinkers on the necks und sleeves is stylish for boys," and he gazed longingly at the neatly embroidered anchors which adorned the sailor suit.

"Oh, yes; suits mit sinkers is awful stylish. They could to cost three dollars. I seen 'em on Grand Street," said Nathan, and Isidore's heart beat high beneath the "sinker" on his breast.

When the first transports of joy over the reunion had abated, Isidore explained his presence and his appearance.

"My mamma," he began proudly, "she sets by the Principal's side und he says, like that, you should come for see my mamma. She's new."

Teacher deftly patted her hair and stock into place, and set out in great interest and excitement to see the "beautiful yonge uptown lady."

"Come, Isidore," she called.

"Mine name ain't Isidore," he announced "Und it ain't Issie neither, but it's awful stylish. I gets it off my new mamma. It's a new name too."

"Dear me," cried Miss Bailey. "What is it, then?"

"I don't know," answered Isidore. "I couldn't to say it even."

"Dear me!" cried Miss Bailey again, and hurried on.

At the door of the Principal's office Teacher halted in puzzled surprise, for the first glance at the glowing face of the new mamma, and the first sound of her pleasant voice, proclaimed, beyond the shadow of a doubt, that Mrs. Lazarus Diamantstein the second was a buxom daughter of the Island of Saints. The little sailor climbed upon her lap, and the Principal introduced the matron to the maid. Miss Bailey said all that etiquette demanded and that interest prompted and Mrs. Diamantstein blushed prettily.

"Thank you kindly," she answered.

"You're very good, but I knew that before. Larry - me husband, you know - often told me how good you were to the child."

"Ah, but you see," said Teacher, "I was very fond of Isidore."

"That's not his name at all, Miss," said Mrs. Diamantstein decidedly. "That's a haythen name, and so I'm going to have him christened. Tell your name to the lady, allannah."

Thus encouraged, Isidore toyed with a diamond stud, not much larger than a butter-plate, which glittered in the new shirtwaist of his new mamma, and uttered a perfectly unintelligible string of sounds.

"See how well he knows it," said the parent proudly. "He says his name is Ignatius Aloysius Diamantstein. Think of him knowing it already and him not christened until next Sunday! I'll have them all christened at once by Father Burke, over at St. Mary's, and I came here to ask you two things. First, knowing the liking you have for the child, I ask you will you be godmother to Ignatius Aloysius?"

Miss Bailey felt unable to cope, all unaided, with these sudden and bewildering changes. Isidore christened and Christianized! Isidore her godchild! She sought inspiration in the Principal, but his shoulders shook with unsympathetic mirth, and his face was turned away. Left to her own puzzled guidance, she answered:

"Really, Mrs. Diamantstein, you are too good. I have

been trying to take care of - of - "

"Ignatius Aloysius," murmured the Principal. "Ye gods, and with that face!"

"Of Ignatius," continued Miss Bailey, stifling a wild inclination towards unseemly laughter, "and I should be delighted to be his godmother, but - but - "

"Well, then, that's settled, and thank you Miss. And now the other thing: Will you take Ignatius Aloysius back into your class? Larry told me how them three children wouldn't go to school for the longest time back, before I was married. Gettin' the little place ready for me, he says they were, and stayin' at home to do it. The darlin's! And lately I was too busy with one thing and another to bring them back. But now I've got Denis and Michael, me other two boys, entered over at the Christian Brothers' school. I was goin' to send the little fellow there too, but he cried to come to you. Won't you take him?"

Miss Bailey appealed to the Principal. "Please," said she, "may I have my godson, Ignatius Aloysius, in my class?"

"I shall try to arrange it so."

Mrs. Diamantstein fixed grateful eyes on Teacher. "You're a good young lady," she repeated, with deep conviction. "And if one of them was a girl I'd call him after you. May I make so bold as to ask your name?"

"Constance."

"Well, now, that's grand. That's a beautiful name.

Himself has two little girls in the orphans' home and I think I'll get one out and call it that. But, maybe, I won't. But anyway, the first one I get I'll call Constance, after you."

When Mrs. Diamantstein had taken her decorous leave of the Principal, Miss Bailey and she walked to the great front door. As they reached it Mrs. Diamantstein reiterated her gratitude and added: "You'll be there at three o'clock, won't you, Miss? For we're to have a grand time at the party after the christening. Father Burke promised to come home to the little place with us, and Larry is goin' round now askin' his friends. And it's the queer owld friends he has, Miss, the queerest ever I seen, and with the queerest owld talk out of them. But sure, the little man will enjoy himself more if he has some of his own at the party."

"And do you mean to tell me that the man is asking his Jewish friends to a Catholic christening?" remonstrated Miss Bailey, who had seen something of the racial antagonism which was rending all that district.

"Sure, not at all, Miss," answered Mrs. Larry reassuringly. "Do you think I'd tell him what the party was for? What does the poor man know about christenings? and him, God help him, a haythen of a Jew. Make your mind easy, Miss; it'll just be a party to him. No more than that."

"But he - all of them - will see Father Burke," Miss Bailey urged.

"And who could they see that would do them more good?" demanded Mrs. Diamantstein belligerently. "Cock them up then. It's not often they'd be let into the one room with a saint of a man like that. They'll likely be the better of it for all the rest of their poor dark days."

Teacher made one more effort towards fair play. "I think," she persisted, "that you ought to tell your husband what you intend to do. It would be dreadful if, after all your trouble, he should not let you change the boys' religion."

"Let, indeed!" cried the bride warmly. "He can wait to do that until he's asked. I'd be long sorry to have a man like that with no bringing up of his own, as you might say, comin' between me and me duty in the sight of God. 'Let,' is it?" And the broad shoulders of Bridget Diamantstein stiffened while her clear eye flashed. "Well, I'm fond enough of that little man, but I'd break his sewin'-machine and dance on his derby before I'd see him bring up the darlin's for black Protestant Jews like himself."

And across the space of many weeks, Mr. Diamantstein's voice rang again in Teacher's ears: "She's a beautiful yonge uptown lady, but easy scared. Oh, awful easy scared!"

Well, love was ever blind.

H.R.H. THE PRINCE OF HESTER STREET

"It will be difficult," said Miss Bailey, gently insubordinate, "very difficult. I have already a register of fifty-eight and seats for only fifty. It is late in the term, too; the children read and write quite easily. And you say this new boy has never been at school?"

"Never," admitted the Principal. "His people are rather distrustful of us. Some religious prejudice, I believe. They are the strictest of the strict. The grandfather is a Rabbi and has been educating the boy - an only child, by the way."

"Put him in the kindergarten," Miss Bailey interjected hopefully.

"No," answered the Principal, "he's too old for that."

"Then let him wait until he can enter with the beginners in September. He will be really unhappy when he finds himself so far behind the others here."

"I'm afraid I must ask you to take him now," the Principal persisted. "His father, the Assemblyman for this district, sees some advantage in sending his boy to school with the children of his supporters. But, of course, I shan't expect you to bring the child up to the grade. Just let him stay here and be happy. If you will send your roll-book to my office I will have him entered."

And so it chanced, on an afternoon of early March, that the name of Isaac Borrachsohn was added - all unalphabetically - at the end of the roll-call of the First Reader Class.

A writing lesson was in progress on the next morning when the new boy arrived. Miss Bailey, during her six months' reign over Room 18, had witnessed many first appearances, but never had charge of hers been borne into court on such a swelling tide of female relatives. The rather diminutive Teacher was engulfed in black-jetted capes, twinkling ear-rings, befeathered hats, warmly gleaming faces, and many flounced skirts, while the devoted eyes of the First Reader Class caught but fleeing glimpses of its sovereign between the red roses rising, quite without visible support, above agitated bonnets.

Against this background Isaac glowed like a bird-of-paradise. The writing lesson halted. Bluntly pointed pencils paused in mid-air or between surprise-parted lips, and the First Reader Class drew deep breaths of awe and admiration: for the new boy wore the brightest and tightest of red velvet Fauntleroy suits, the most bouffant of underlying shirts, the deepest of lace collars, the most straightly cut of Anglo-Saxon coiffures, the most far-reaching of sailor hats. Sadie Gonorowsky, the haughty Sadie, paused open-eyed in her distribution of writing papers. Morris Mogilewsky, the gentle Morris, abstractedly bit off and swallowed a piece of the gold-fish food. Isidore Belchatosky, the exquisite Isidore, passed a stealthy hand over his closely cropped red head and knew that his reign was over.

Miss Bailey determined, in view of the frightened expression in the new-comer's eyes, to forgive his inopportune enlistment. At her cordial words of welcome the alarm spread from his wide eyes to his trembling lips, and Teacher turned to the relatives to ask: "Doesn't he speak English?"

There ensued much babbling and gesticulation. Isaac was volubly reproved, and then one of the younger and befeathered aunts made answer.

"Sure does he. Only he was bashful, and when he should get sooner over it he English just like you speaks. Just like you he speaks. He is a good boy. Where is he goin' to sit? Where is his place?"

Miss Bailey reflected with dismay that there was not an unassigned desk in the room. Fortunately, however, Patrick Brennan was absent on that morning - he was "making the mission" at St. Mary's church with his mother - and his queer assortment of string, buttons, pencil stumps, and a mute and battered mouth-organ, were swept into a drawer of Teacher's desk. Isaac was installed in this hastily created vacancy, the gratified relatives withdrew, and the writing lesson was resumed.

When Isaac found himself cut entirely away from the maternal apron-strings, his impulse was towards the relief of tears, but his wandering gaze encountered the admiring eyes of Eva Gonorowsky and his aimless hand came in contact with the hidden store of chewing-gum with which the absent Patrick was won't to refresh himself, lightly attached to the under surface of the chair. Isaac promptly applied it to the soothing of his spirits, and decided that a school which furnished such dark and curly locked neighbours and such delectable sustenance was a pleasant place. So he accepted a long pencil from Sarah Schrodsky, and a sheet of paper from Sadie Gonorowsky, and fell to copying the writing on the board.

While he laboured - quite unsuccessfully, since all his grandsire's instructions had been in Hebrew - Miss Bailey passed from desk to desk on a tour of inspection and exhortation, slightly annoyed and surprised to find that the excitement consequent upon Isaac Borrachsohn's introduction had not yet subsided. Eva Gonorowsky was flagrantly inattentive, and Teacher paused to point an accusing finger at the very erratic markings which she had achieved.

"Eva," said she, "why do you keep your writing so very far from the line?"

"I ain't so big," Eva responded meekly, "und so I makes mistakes. I tells you 'scuse."

"Honey," responded Miss Bailey, her wrath quite turned away by this soft answer, "you could do beautifully if you would only look at the board instead of staring at the new boy."

"Yiss ma'am," acquiesced Eva. "But, oh, Teacher, Missis Bailey, *ain't* he the sweet dude!"

"Do you think so? Well, you need not stop writing to look at him, because you will be seeing him every day.

"In this class? Oh, ain't that fine!" Eva whispered.

"My, ain't his mamma put him on nice mit red-from-plush suits and stylish hair-cuts!"

"Well, Isidore Belchatosky has a velvet suit," said the gentle-hearted Miss Bailey, as she noticed the miserable eyes of the deposed beau travelling from his own frayed sleeve to the scarlet splendour across the aisle.

"But's it's black," sneered the small coquette, and Teacher was only just in time to snatch Isidore's faultless writing from the deluge of his bitter tears.

When the First Reader Class filed down the yard for recess, Miss Bailey was disgusted to find that Isaac Borrachsohn's admiring audience increased until it included every boy in the school young enough to be granted these twenty minutes of relaxation during the long morning. He was led away to a distant corner, there to receive tribute of deference, marbles, candy, tops, and political badges. But he spoke no word. Silently and gravely he held court. Gravely and silently he suffered himself to be led back to Room 18. Still silently and still gravely he went home at twelve o'clock.

At a quarter before one on that day, while Morris Mogilewsky and Nathan Spiderwitz, Monitors of Gold-Fish and Window Boxes, were waiting dejectedly for the opening of the school doors and reflecting that they must inevitably find themselves supplanted in their sovereign's regard - for Teacher, though an angel, was still a woman, and therefore sure to prefer gorgeously arrayed ministers - there entered to them Patrick Brennan, fortified by the morning's devotion, and reacting sharply against the morning's restraint.

"Fellars," he began jubilantly; "I know where we can hook a banana. And the Ginney's asleep. Come on!"

His colleagues looked at him with lack-lustre eyes. "I don't need no bananas," said Morris dispiritedly. "They ain't so awful healthy fer me."

"Me too," Nathan agreed. "I et six once und they made me a sickness."

"Bananas!" urged Patrick. "Bananas, an' the man asleep! What's the matter with ye anyway?"

"There's a new boy in our class," Morris answered. "Und he's a dude. Und Teacher's lovin' mit him."

"Und he sets in your place," added Nathan.

"I'll break his face if he tries it again," cried Patrick hotly. "Who let him sit there?"

"Teacher," wailed Morris. "Ain't I tell you how she's lovin' mit him?"

"And where's all *my* things?" Patrick demanded with pardonable curiosity. "Where am I to sit?"

"She makes you should set by her side," Morris reassured him. "Und keep your pencil in her desk. It could be awful nice fer you. You sets right by her."

"I'll try it for a day or two," said Patrick grandly. "I'll see how I'll like it."

For the first hour he liked it very well. It was fun to sit beside Miss Bailey, to read from her reader, to write at her desk, to look grandly down upon his fellows, and to smile with condescension upon Eva Gonorowsky. But when Teacher opened her book of Fairy Tales and led the way to the land of magic Patrick discovered that the chewing gum, with which he was accustomed to refresh himself on these journeys, was gone. Automatically he swept his hand across the under surface of his chair. It was not there. He searched the drawer in which his treasures had been bestowed. Nor there. He glanced at the usurper in his rightful place, and saw that the jaws of Isaac moved rhythmically and placidly. Hot anger seized Patrick. He rose deliberately upon his sturdy legs and slapped the face of that sweet dude so exactly and with such force that the sound broke upon the quiet air like the crack of a revolver. Teacher, followed by the First Reader Class, rushed back from Fairy Land, and the next few minutes were devoted to separating the enraged Patrick from the terrified Isaac, who, in the excitement of the onslaught, had choked upon the *casus belli*, and could make neither restitution nor explanation. When Isaac was reduced, at the cost of much time and petting on Miss Bailey's part, to that stage of consolation in which departing grief takes the form of loud sobs, closely resembling hiccoughs and as surprising to the sufferer as to his sympathizers, Patrick found himself in universal disfavour. The eyes of the boys, always so loyal, were cold. The eyes of the girls, always so admiring, were reproachful. The eyes of Miss Bailey, always so loving, were hard and angry. Teacher professed herself too grieved and surprised to continue the interrupted story, and Patrick was held responsible for the substitution of a brisk mental arithmetic test in which he was easily distanced by every boy and girl in the room. But Isaac was still silent. No halcyon suggestion beginning, "Suppose I were to give you a dollar and you spent half of it for candy," no imaginary shopping orgie, could tempt him into speech.

It was nearly three o'clock when at last he found his voice. In an idle inspection of his new desk he came upon one of those combinations of a pen, a pencil, and an eraser, which gladden the young and aggravate the old. It was one of Patrick's greatest treasures and had long been Eva's envious desire, and now Patrick, chained to the side of his indignant Teacher, saw this precious, delicate, and stubborn mechanism at the mercy of his clumsy successor. Isaac wrenched and twisted without avail; Patrick's wrath grew dark; Eva shyly proffered assistance; Patrick's jealousy flamed hot. And then, before Patrick's enraged eyes, Eva and Isaac tore the combination of writing implements to fragments, in their endeavour to make it yield a point. Patrick darted upon the surprised Isaac like an avenging whirlwind, and drove a knotty little fist into the centre of the Fauntleroy costume. And then, quite suddenly, Isaac lifted up his voice:

"Don't you dast to touch me," he yelled, "you - Krisht fool."

Miss Bailey sprang to her feet, but before she could reach the offender he had warmed to his work and was rolling off excerpts from remarks which he had heard at his father's club-rooms. These were, of course, in Hebrew, but after much hissing and many gutturals, he arrived, breathless, at the phrase as Anglo-Saxon as his hair:

"You be - ! Go to - !"

Of all Miss Bailey's rules for the government of her

kingdom the most stringent were against blasphemy. Never had her subjects seen their gentle lady so instinct with wrath as she was when holding the wriggling arm of Patrick with one hand and the red plush shoulder of Isaac with the other, she resumed her place in the chair of authority. She leaned forward until her eyes, angry and determined, were looking close into Patrick's, and began:

"You first. You commenced this thing. Now listen. If you ever touch that boy again - I don't care for what reason - I will whip you. Here, before the whole class, I shall spank you. Do you understand?"

"Yes," said Patrick.

"And now you," turning quickly to Isaac. "If you ever again dare to say bad words in this room I shall wash out the mouth you soil in saying them. Do you understand?"

Isaac was silent.

"Do you understand?" repeated Miss Bailey. Isaac spoke no word; gave no sign of comprehension.

"Morris," called Teacher, "come and tell him that in Jewish for me," and Morris, with many halts and shy recoilings, whispered a few words into the ear of Isaac, who remonstrated volubly.

"He says he ain't said no bad word," the interpreter explained. "His papa says like that on his mamma, and his mamma says like that on his papa. Fer him, that ain't no bad word."

"It is a bad word here," said Teacher inexorably. "Tell him I'll wash out his mouth if he says it again."

Miss Bailey was so ruffled and disgusted by the course of events that she allowed only the Monitor of the Gold-Fish Bowl to stay with her after school that afternoon. When readers were counted and put upon shelves, charts furled, paint brushes washed, pencils sharpened, and blackboards cleaned, Morris pressed close to his lady and whispered:

"Say, Teacher, I should tell you somethings."

"Well, then, old man, tell it."

"Teacher, it's like this; I ain't tell Ikey, out of Jewish, how you says you should wash out his mouth."

"You didn't tell him? And why not, pray?"

"Well," and Morris's tone, though apologetic, was self-righteous, "I guess you don't know about Ikey Borrachsohn."

"I know he said two very bad things. Of course, I did not understand the Jewish part. What did he say? Did you know?"

"Sure did I, on'y I wouldn't to tell it out. It ain't fer you. It ain't no fer-ladies word."

Miss Bailey patted her small knight's hand. "Thank you, Morris," she said simply. "And so it was bad?"

"Fierce."

"Very well; I shall ask some other boy to tell him that I shall wash out his mouth."

"Well," Morris began as before, "I guess you don't know 'bout Isaac Borrachsohn. You dassent to wash out his mouth, 'cause his grandpa's a Rabbi."

"I know he is. Is that any reason for Isaac's swearing?"

"His papa," Morris began in an awed whisper, "his papa's the King of Hester Street."

"Well," responded Teacher calmly, "that makes no difference to me. No one may swear in this room. And now, Morris, you must run home. Your mother will be wondering where you are."

Three minutes later Morris's dark head reappeared. His air was deeply confidential. "Teacher, Missis Bailey," he began, "I tells you 'scuse."

"Well, dear, what is it?" asked Miss Bailey with divided interest, as she adjusted a very large hat with the guidance of a very small looking-glass. "What do you want?"

Again Morris hesitated. "I guess," he faltered; "I guess you don't know 'bout Isaac Borrachsohn."

"What has happened to him? Is he hurt?"

"It's his papa. Ain't I told you he's the King of Hester Street und he's got dancing balls. My mamma und all the ladies on our block they puts them on stylish und goes on the ball. Und ain't you see how he's got a stylish mamma mit di'monds on the hair?"

"Yes," admitted Miss Bailey, "I saw the diamonds." Not to have seen the paste buckle which menaced Mrs. Borrachsohn's left eye would have been to be blind indeed.

"Und extra, you says you should wash out his mouth," Morris remonstrated. "I guess, maybe, you fools."

"You'll see," said Miss Bailey blithely. "And now trot along, my dear. Good afternoon."

Teacher hurried into her jacket and was buttoning her gloves when the Monitor of the Gold-Fish Bowl looked timidly in.

"What now?" asked Teacher.

"Well," said Morris, and breathed hard,

"I guess you don't know 'bout Isaac Borrachsohn."

Miss Bailey fell away into helpless laughter. "That would not be your fault, honey, even if it were true," she said. "But what has he been doing since I saw you?"

"It's his papa," answered Morris. "His papa's got p'rades."

"He has what?"

"P'rades."

"And are they very bad? I never heard of them."

"You don't know what is p'rades?" cried Morris.

"Won't your mamma leave you see them?"

"What are they?" asked Teacher. "Did you ever see them?"

"Sure I seen p'rades. My papa he takes me in his hand und I stands by the curb und looks on the p'rade. It goes by night. Comes mans und comes cops und comes George Wash'ton und comes Ikey Borrachsohn's papa, mit proud looks - he makes polite bows mit his head on all the peoples, und comes Teddy Rosenfelt. Und comes cows und more cops und ladies und el'fints, und comes Captain Dreyfus und Terry McGovern. Und comes mans, und mans, und mans - a great big all of mans - und they says: 'What's the matter with Ikey Borrachsohn's papa?' - he ain't got no sickness, Miss Bailey, on'y it's polite you say like that on p'rades. Und more mans they says: 'Nothings is mit him. He's all right!' That is what is p'rades. Ikey's papa's got them, und so you *dassent* to wash out his mouth."

"One more bad word," was Teacher's ultimatum; "one more and then I'll do it."

Miss Bailey's commands were not lightly disregarded, and Patrick Brennan spent the ensuing week in vain endeavour to reconcile himself to a condition of things in which he, the first born of the policeman on the beat, and therefore by right of heredity a person of importance in the realm, should tamely submit to usurpation and insult on the part of this mushroom sprig of moneyed aristocracy, this sissy kid in velvet pants, this long-haired dummy of an Isaac Borrachsohn. Teacher could not have meant to cut him off from all hope of vengeance. If she had - then she must be shown that the honour of the house of Brennan was a thing beyond even her jurisdiction. A Brennan had been insulted in his person and in his property. Of course, he must have satisfaction.

If Morris could have known that Patrick, of whom he was so fond, was plotting evil against the heir-apparent to the throne of Hester Street, he might have persuaded that scion of the royal house of Munster to stay his hand. But the advice of Patrick pere had always been: "Lay low until you see a good chanst, an' then sock it to 'em good and plenty." So Patrick fils bided his time and continued to "make the mission" with his pious mother.

After his initial speech in his English, so like Miss Bailey's, Isaac Borrachsohn resumed his cloak of silence and spoke no more of the language of the land. Even in his own tongue he was far from garrulous. And yet his prestige continued to increase, his costumes grew ever more gorgeous, and his slaves - both male and female - daily more numerous. In reading and in "Memory Gems" his progress was, under the veil of speechlessness, imperceptible, but in writing and in all the prescribed branches of Manual Training he acquired a proficiency which made it impossible to return him to his royal sire. Gradually it was borne in upon Miss Bailey that she had met her Waterloo - a child who would have none of her. All her attempts at friendliness were met by the same stolid silence, the same impersonal regard, until in desperation, she essayed a small store of German phrases, relics of her sophomore days. Six faulty sentences, with only the most remote bearing upon the subject in hand, were more efficacious than volumes of applied psychology, and the reserve of Isaac

Borrachsohn vanished before the rising conviction that Teacher belonged to his own race. How otherwise, he demanded, could she speak such beautiful Hebrew? When Morris translated this tribute to Patrick, a flame of anger and of hope lit up that Celtic soul. Such an accusation brought against Miss Bailey, whom he had heard his noble father describe as "one of ourselves, God bless her!" was bitter to hear, but the Knight of Munster comforted himself with the conviction that Teacher would no longer shield the sissy from the retribution he now had doubly earned. But it should be a retribution fitted to the offender and in proportion to the offence. Long experience of Jewish playfellows had taught Patrick a revenge more fiendish than a beating, a ducking, a persecution by "de gang," or a confiscation of goods and treasures. All of these were possible and hard to bear, but for Isaac's case something worse was needed. He should be branded with a cross! Fortune, after weeks of frowning, was with Patrick on that warm April afternoon. Isaac was attired in a white linen costume so short of stocking and of knickerbockers as to exhibit surprising area of fat leg, so fashionable in its tout ensemble as to cause Isidore Belchatosky to weep aloud, so spotless as to prompt Miss Bailey to shield it with her own "from silk" apron when the painting lesson commenced. Patrick Brennan had obeyed his father's injunction to "lay low" so carefully that Teacher granted a smiling assent to his plea to be allowed to occupy the place, which chanced to be empty, immediately behind Isaac's.

On each little desk Miss Bailey, assisted by her whole corps of monitors, placed a sheet of drawing paper, a little pan containing India ink dissolved in water, and a fat Japanese paint brush. The class was delighted, for, with the possible exception of singing, there was no more popular occupation. Briskly the First Reader Class fell to work. Carefully they dipped brushes in ink. Bravely they commenced to draw. Teacher passed from desk to desk encouraging the timid, restraining the rash.

Patrick dug his brush deep down into his ink, lifted it all wet and dripping, cast a furtive glance at Teacher's averted head, and set stealthily to work at the bent and defenceless back of Isaac Borrachsohn's spotless suit. From shoulder to shoulder he drew a thick black mark. Then another from straight cropped hair to patent leather belt. Mrs. Borrachsohn belonged to the school of mothers who believed in winter underwear until the first of June, and Isaac felt nothing. But Eva Gonorowsky saw and shuddered, hiding her eyes from the symbol and the desecration. Patrick glowered at her, filled his brush again, bent quickly down, and branded the bare and mottled legs of his enemy with two neatly crossed strokes.

In an instant the room was in an uproar. Patrick, his face and hands daubed with ink, was executing a triumphant war-dance around Isaac, who, livid and inarticulate with rage, was alternately struggling for words and making wondrous Delsartean attempts to see his outraged back.

"I socked it to you good and plenty!" chanted Patrick in shrill victory. "Look at your back! Look at your leg! It's ink! It won't come off! It will never come off! Look at your back!"

Miss Bailey clanged the bell, caught Patrick by the waist-line, thrust him under her desk, fenced him in with a chair, and turned to Isaac who had only just realized the full horror of his plight. Isidore Belchatosky and Eva Gonorowsky had torn off the white tunic - thereby disclosing quantities of red flannel - and exhibited its desecrated back. And speech, English speech returned to the Prince of Hester Street. Haltingly at first, but with growing fluency he cursed and swore and blasphemed; using words of whose existence Teacher had never heard or known and at whose meaning she could but faintly guess. Eva began to whimper; Nathan lifted shocked eyes to Teacher; Patrick kicked away the barricading chair and, still armed with the inky brush, sprang into the arena, and it was not until five minutes later that gentle peace settled down on Room 18.

Miss Bailey had received full parental authority from the policeman on the beat and she felt that the time for its exercise had come.

"Patrick," she commanded. "Position!" And the Leader of the Line stood forth stripped of his rank and his followers, but not of his dauntless bearing.

Teacher, with a heavy heart, selected the longest and lightest of her rulers and the review continued.

"Hips firm!" was the next command, and Patrick's grimy hands sprang to his hips.

"Trunk forward - bend!" Patrick doubled like a jack-knife and Miss Bailey did her duty.

When it was over she was more distressed than was her victim. "Patrick, I'm so sorry this happened," said she. "But you remember that I warned you that I should whip you if you touched Isaac. Well, you did and I did. You know - all the children know - that I always keep my word."

"Yiss ma'an," murmured the frightened First Reader Class.

"Always?" asked Patrick.

"Always," said Miss Bailey.

"Then wash out his mouth," said Patrick, pointing to the gloating Isaac, who promptly ceased from gloating.

"Oh, that reminds me," cried Teacher, "of something I want you to do. Will you tell Isaac you are sorry for spoiling his new suit?"

"Sure," answered Patrick readily. "Say, Isaac, I'm sorry. Come and git your mouth washed."

"Well," Miss Bailey temporized, "his clothes are ruined. Don't you think you could forgive him without the washing?"

"Sure," answered Patrick again. "Ain't it too bad that you can't, too! But you said it and now you've got to do it. Like you did about me, you know. Where's the basin? I'll fill it."

Teacher was fairly trapped, but, remembering that Isaac's provocation had been great, she determined to make the ordeal as bearable as possible. She sent for some water, selected a piece of appetizing rose pink soap, a relic of her Christmas store, and called Isaac, who, when he guessed the portent of all these preliminaries, suffered a shocking relapse into English. Nerved by this latest exhibition, Miss Bailey was deaf to the wails of Isaac and unyielding to the prayers and warnings of Morris and to the frantic sympathy of Eva Gonorowsky.

"Soap ain't fer us," Morris cried. "It ain't fer us. We don't ever make like you makes mit soap!"

"I noticed that," said Teacher dryly. "I really think you are afraid of soap and water. When I finish with Isaac you will all see how good it is for boys and girls to be washed."

"But not in the mouth! Oh, Missis Bailey, soap in the mouth ain't fer us."

"Nonsense, honey," answered Teacher; "it will only clean his teeth and help him to remember not to say nasty words." And, all unaware of the laws of "kosher" and of "traef," the distinctions between clean and unclean, quite as rigorous as, and much more complicated than, her own, Constance Bailey washed out the mouth of her royal charge, and, it being then three o'clock, dismissed her awed subjects and went serenely home.

On his progress towards the palace of his sire, Isaac Borrachsohn, with Christian symbols printed large upon his person, alienated nine loyal Hebrew votes from his father's party and collected a following of small boys which nearly blocked the narrow streets. The crosses were bad enough, but when it was made clear that the contamination, in the form of bright pink soap, had penetrated to the innermost recesses of the heir of the Barrachsohns, the aunts, in frozen horror, turned for succour and advice to the Rabbi. But he could only confirm their worst fears. "Soap," said he, "is from the fat of pigs. Our boy is defiled. To-morrow he must be purified at the synagogue. I told you it was a Christian school."

Then did the Assemblyman quail before the reproach of his women. Then did he bite his nails in indecision and remorse and swear to be revenged upon the woman who had dared so to pollute his son. Then did Isaac weep continuously, noisily, but ineffectually for, on the morrow, to the synagogue he went.

Miss Bailey, when she saw that he was absent, was mildly self-reproachful and uneasy. If she could have known of the long and complicated rites and services which she had brought upon the boy who had been entrusted to her to be kept happy and out of mischief, she might not have listened so serenely to the janitor's announcement two days later.

"Borrachsohn and a whole push of women, and an old bird with a beard, are waitin' for you in the boys' yard," he whispered with great *empressement*. "I sent them there," he explained, "because they wouldn't fit anywhere else. There's about a hundred of them."

Mr. Borrachsohn's opening remark showed that the force of Isaac's speech was hereditary. "Are you the - young woman who's been playing such fool tricks with my son? You'll wish you minded your own - business before I get through with you."

The belligerent attitude was reflected by the phalanx of female relatives, whose red roses waved in defiance now, as they had nodded in amity a few short weeks before. For an instant Teacher did not grasp the full meaning of Mr. Borrachsohn's greeting. Then suddenly she realized that this man, this trafficker in the blood and the honour of his people, had dared to swear at her, Constance Bailey. When her eyes met those of the Assemblyman he started slightly, and placed Isaac between him and this alarming young person who seemed not at all to realize that he could "break her" with a word.

"Is this your child?" she demanded. And he found himself answering meekly:

"Yes ma'an."

"Then take him away," she commanded. "He is not fit to be with decent children. I refuse to teach him."

"You can't refuse," said Mr. Borrachsohn. "It is the law - "

"Law!" repeated Teacher. "What is the law to you?" She was an open-eyed young person; she had spent some months in Mr. Borrachsohn's district; she had a nasty energy of phrase; and the King of Hester Street has never translated the ensuing remarks to the wife of his bosom nor to the gentle-eyed old Rabbi who watched, greatly puzzled by his ideal of a Christian persecutor and this very different reality. Gradually the relatives saw that the accuser had become the accused, but they were hardly prepared to see him supplicating and even unsuccessfully.

"No, I won't take him. I tell you his language is awful. I can't let the other children hear him."

"But I shall see that he swears no more. We taught him for a joke. I'll stop him."

"I'm afraid you can't."

"Well, you try him. Try him for two weeks. He is a good boy; he will swear no more."

"Very well," was Teacher's ungracious acquiescence; "I shall try him again. And if he should swear - "

"You will not wash out his mouth - "

"I shall, and this time I shall use hot water and sapolio and washing soda."

Mr. Borrachsohn smiled blandly and turned to explain this dictum to his clan. And the dazed Miss Bailey saw the anger and antagonism die out of the faces before her and the roses above them, heard Mr. Borrachsohn's gentle, "We would be much obliged if you will so much accommodate us," saw the Rabbi lift grateful eyes to the ceiling and clasp his hands, saw Mrs. Borrachsohn brush away a tear of joy, and felt Isaac's soft and damp little palm placed within her own by the hand of his royal sire, saw the jetted capes, the flounced skirts, and befeathered hats follow the blue and brass buttons of the janitor, the broadcloth of the Assemblyman and the alpaca of the Rabbi, heard the door close with a triumphant bang, saw the beaming face of the returning janitor, and heard his speech of congratulation:

"I heard it all; I was afraid to leave you alone with them. Will you excuse me, Miss Bailey, if I just pass the remark that you're a living wonder?"

Still densely puzzled and pondering as to whether she could hope ever to understand these people, she sought the Principal and told him the whole story. "And now why," she asked, "did he make such a fuss about the washing only to yield without a struggle at the end?"

The Principal laughed. "You are mistaken," said he. "Mr. Borrachsohn gained his point and you most gracefully capitulated."

"I," cried Teacher; "I yield to that horrid man! Never! I said I should use soda and sapolio - "

"Precisely," the Principal acquiesced. "And both soda and sapolio are kosher - lawful, clean. Miss Bailey, oh, Miss Bailey, you can never be haughty and lofty again, for you met 'that horrid man' in open battle and went weakly down before him."

THE LAND OF HEART'S DESIRE

Isaac Borrachsohn, that son of potentates and of Assemblymen, had been taken to Central Park by a proud uncle. For weeks thereafter he was the favourite bard of the First Reader Class and an exceeding great trouble to its sovereign, Miss Bailey, who found him now as garrulous as he had once been silent. There was no subject in the Course of Study to which he could not correlate the wonders of his journey, and Teacher asked herself daily and in vain whether it were more pedagogically correct to encourage "spontaneous self-expression" or to insist upon "logically essential sequence."

But the other members of the class suffered no such uncertainty. They voted solidly for spontaneity in a self which found expression thus:

"Und in the Central Park stands a water-lake, und in the water-lake stands birds - a big all of birds - und fishes. Und sooner you likes you should come over the water-lake you calls a bird, und you sets on the bird, und the bird makes go his legs, und you comes over the water-lake."

"They could to be awful polite birds," Eva Gonorowsky was beginning when Morris interrupted with:

"I had once a auntie und she had a bird, a awful polite bird; on'y sooner somebody calls him he *couldn't* to come the while he sets in a cage."

"Did he have a rubber neck?" Isaac inquired, and Morris reluctantly admitted that he had not been so blessed.

"In the Central Park," Isaac went on, "all the birds is got rubber necks."

"What colour from birds be they?" asked Eva.

"All colours. Blue und white und red und yellow."

"Und green," Patrick Brennan interjected determinedly. "The green ones is the best."

"Did you go once?" asked Isaac, slightly disconcerted.

"Naw, but I know. Me big brother told me."

"They could to be stylish birds, too," said Eva wistfully. "Stylish und polite. From red und green birds is awful stylish for hats."

"But these birds is big. Awful big! Mans could to ride on 'em und ladies und boys."

"Und little girls, Ikey? Ain't they fer little girls?" asked the only little girl in the group. And a very small girl she was, with a softly gentle voice and darkly gentle eyes fixed pleadingly now upon the bard.

"Yes," answered Isaac grudgingly; "sooner they sets by somebody's side little girls could to go. But sooner nobody holds them by the hand they could to have fraids over the rubber-neck-boat-birds und the water-lake, und the fishes."

"What kind from fishes?" demanded Morris Mogilewsky, Monitor of Miss Bailey's Gold-Fish Bowl, with professional interest.

"From gold fishes und red fishes und black fishes" - Patrick stirred uneasily and Isaac remembered - "und green fishes; the green ones is the biggest; und blue fishes und *all* kinds from fishes. They lives way down in the water the while they have fraids over the rubber-neck-boat-birds. Say, what you think? Sooner a rubber-neck-boat-bird needs he should eat he longs down his neck und eats a from gold fish."

"'Out fryin'?" asks Eva, with an incredulous shudder.

"Yes, 'out fryin'. Ain't I told you little girls could to have fraids over 'em? Boys could to have fraids too," cried Isaac; and then spurred on by the calm of his rival, he added: "The rubber-neck-boat-birds they hollers somethin' fierce."

"I wouldn't be afraid of them. Me pop's a cop," cried Patrick stoutly. "I'd just as lief set on 'em. I'd like to."

"Ah, but you ain't seen 'em, und you ain't heard 'em holler," Isaac retorted.

"Well, I'm goin' to. An' I'm goin' to see the lions an' the tigers an' the el'phants, an' I'm goin' to ride on the water-lake."

"Oh, how I likes I should go too!" Eva broke out.

O-o-oh, *how* I likes I should look on them things! On'y I don't know do I need a ride on somethings what hollers. I don't know be they fer me."

"Well, I'll take ye with me if your mother leaves you go," said Patrick grandly. "An' ye can hold me hand if ye're scared."

"Me too?" implored Morris. "Oh, Patrick, c'n I go too?"

"I guess so," answered the Leader of the Line graciously. But he turned a deaf ear to Isaac Borrachsohn's implorings to be allowed to join the party. Full well did Patrick know of the grandeur of Isaac's holiday attire and the impressionable nature of Eva's soul, and gravely did he fear that his own Sunday finery, albeit fashioned from the blue cloth and brass buttons of his sire, might be outshone.

At Eva's earnest request, Sadie, her cousin, was invited, and Morris suggested that the Monitor of the Window Boxes should not be slighted by his colleagues of the goldfish and the line. So Nathan Spiderwitz was raised to Alpine heights of anticipation by visions of a window box "as big as blocks and streets," where every plant, in contrast to his lanky charges, bore innumerable blossoms. Ignatius Aloysius Diamantstein was unanimously nominated a member of the expedition; by Patrick, because they were neighbours at St. Mary's Sunday-school; by Morris, because they were classmates under the same Rabbi at the synagogue; by Nathan, because Ignatius Aloysius was a member of the "Clinton Street gang"; by Sadie, because he had "long pants sailor suit"; by Eva, because the others wanted him.

Eva reached home that afternoon tingling with anticipation and uncertainty. What if her mother, with one short word, should close forever the gates of joy and boat-birds? But Mrs. Gonorowsky met her small daughter's elaborate plea with the simple question:

"Who pays you the car-fare?"

"Does it need car-fare to go?" faltered Eva.

"Sure does it," answered her mother. "I don't know how much, but some it needs. Who pays it?"

"Patrick ain't said."

"Well, you should better ask him," Mrs. Gonorowsky advised, and, on the next morning, Eva did. She thereby buried the leader under the ruins of his fallen castle of clouds, but he struggled through them with the suggestion that each of his guests should be her, or his, own banker.

"But ain't you got *no* money 't all?" asked the guest of honour.

"Not a cent," responded the host. "But I'll get it. How much have you?"

"A penny. How much do I need?"

"I don't know. Let's ask Miss Bailey."

School had not yet formally begun and Teacher was reading. She was hardly disturbed when the children drove sharp elbows into her shoulder and her lap, and she answered Eva's - "Missis Bailey - oh, Missis

Bailey," with an abstracted - "Well dear?"

"Missis Bailey, how much money takes car-fare to the Central Park?"

Still with divided attention, Teacher replied - "Five cents, honey," and read on, while Patrick called a meeting of his forces and made embarrassing explanations with admirable tact.

There ensued weeks of struggle and economy for the exploring party, to which had been added a chaperon in the large and reassuring person of Becky Zalmonowsky, the class idiot. Sadie Gonorowsky's careful mother had considered Patrick too immature to bear the whole responsibility, and he, with a guile which promised well for his future, had complied with her desires and preserved his own authority unshaken. For Becky, poor child, though twelve years old and of an aspect eminently calculated to inspire trust in those who had never heldspeech with her, was a member of the First Reader Class only until such time as room could be found for her in some of the institutions where such unfortunates are bestowed.

Slowly and in diverse ways each of the children acquired the essential nickel. Some begged, some stole, some gambled, some bartered, some earned, but their greatest source of income, Miss Bailey, was denied to them. For Patrick knew that she would have insisted upon some really efficient guardian from a higher class, and he announced with much heat that he would not go at all under those circumstances.

At last the leader was called upon to set a day and appointed a Saturday in late May. He was disconcerted to find that only Ignatius Aloysius would travel on that day.

"It's holidays, all Saturdays," Morris explained; "und we dassent to ride on no cars."

"Why not?" asked Patrick.

"It's law, the Rabbi says," Nathan supplemented. "I don't know why is it; on'y rides on holidays ain't fer us."

"I guess," Eva sagely surmised; "I guess rubber-neck-boat-birds rides even ain't fer us on holidays. But I don't know do I need rides on birds what hollers."

"You'll be all right," Patrick assured her. "I'm goin' to let ye hold me hand. If ye can't go on Saturday, I'll take ye on Sunday - next Sunday. Yous all must meet me here on the school steps. Bring yer money and bring yer lunch too. It's a long way and ye'll be hungry when ye get there. Ye get a terrible long ride for five cents."

"Does it take all that to get there?" asked the practical Nathan. "Then how are we goin' to get back?"

Poor little poet soul! Celtic and improvident! Patrick's visions had shown him only the triumphant arrival of his host and the beatific joy of Eva as she floated by his side on the most "fancy" of boat-birds. Of the return journey he had taken no thought. And so the saving and planning had to be done all over again. The struggle for the first nickel had been wearing and wearying, but the amassment of the second was beyond description difficult. The children were worn from long strife and many sacrifices, for the temptations to spend six or nine cents are so much more insistent and unusual than are yearnings to squander lesser sums. Almost daily some member of the band would confess a fall from grace and solvency, and almost daily Isaac Borrachsohn was called upon to descant anew upon the glories of the Central Park. Becky, the chaperon, was the most desultory collector of the party. Over and over she reached the proud heights of seven or even eight cents only to lavish her horde on the sticky joys of the candy cart of Isidore Belchatosky's papa or on the suddy charms of a strawberry soda.

Then tearfully would she repent of her folly, and bitterly would the others upbraid her, telling again of the joys and wonders she had squandered. Then loudly would she bewail her weakness and plead in extenuation: "I seen the candy. Mouses from choc'late und Foxy Gran'pas from sugar - und I ain't never seen no Central Park."

"But don't you know how Isaac says?" Eva would urge. "Don't you know how all things what is nice fer us stands in the Central Park? Say, Isaac, you should better tell Becky, some more, how the Central Park stands."

And Isaac's tales grew daily more wild and independent of fact until the little girls quivered with yearning terror and the boys burnished up forgotten cap pistols. He told of lions, tigers, elephants, bears and buffaloes, all of enormous size and strength of lung, so that before many days had passed he had debarred himself, by whole-hearted lying, from the very possibility of joining the expedition and seeing the disillusionment of his public. With true artistic spirit he omitted all mention of confining house or cage and bestowed the gift of speech upon all the characters, whether brute or human, in his epic. The merry-go-round he combined with the menagerie into a whole which was not to be resisted.

"Und all the am'blins," he informed his entranced listeners; "they goes around, und around, und around, where music plays und flags is. Und I sets on a lion und he runs around, und runs around, und runs around. Say - what you think? He has smiling looks und hair on the neck, und sooner he says like that 'I'm awful thirsty,' I gives him a peanut und I gets a golden ring."

"Where is it?" asked the jealous and incredulous Patrick.

"To my house." Isaac valiantly lied, for well he remembered the scene in which his scandalized but sympathetic uncle had discovered his attempt to purloin the brass ring which, with countless blackened duplicates, is plucked from a slot by the brandishing swords of the riders upon the merry-go-round. Truly, its possession had won him another ride - this time upon an elephant with upturned trunk and wide ears - but in his mind the return of that ring still rankled as the only grief in an otherwise perfect day.

Miss Bailey - ably assisted by Aesop, Rudyard Kipling, and Thompson Seton - had prepared the First Reader Class to accept garrulous and benevolent lions, cows, panthers, and elephants, and the exploring party's absolute credulity encouraged Isaac to higher and yet higher flights, until Becky was strengthened against temptation.

At last, on a Sunday in late June, the cavalcade in splendid raiment met on the wide steps, boarded a Grand Street car, and set out for Paradise. Some confusion occurred at the very beginning of things when Becky Zalmonowsky curtly refused to share her pennies with the conductor. When she was at last persuaded to yield, an embarrassing five minutes was consumed in searching for the required amount in the nooks and crannies of her costume where, for safe-keeping, she had cached her fund. One penny was in her shoe, another in her stocking, two in the lining of her hat, and one in the large and dilapidated chatelaine bag which dangled at her knees.

Nathan Spiderwitz, who had preserved absolute silence, now contributed his fare, moist and warm, from his mouth, and Eva turned to him admonishingly.

"Ain't Teacher told you money in the mouth ain't healthy fer you?" she sternly questioned, and Nathan, when he had removed other pennies, was able to answer:

"I washed 'em first off." And they were indeed most brightly clean. "There's holes in me these here pockets," he explained, and promptly corked himself anew with currency.

"But they don't tastes nice, do they?" Morris remonstrated. Nathan shook a corroborative head. "Und," the Monitor of the Gold-Fish further urged, "you could to swallow 'em und then you couldn't never to come by your house no more."

But Nathan was not to be dissuaded, even when the impressional and experimental Becky tried his storage system and suffered keen discomfort before her penny was restored to her by a resourceful fellow-traveller who thumped her right lustily on the back until her crowings ceased and the coin was once more in her hand.

At the meeting of Grand Street with the Bowery, wild confusion was made wilder by the addition of seven small persons armed with transfers and clamouring - all except Nathan - for Central Park. Two newsboys and a policeman bestowed them upon a Third Avenue car and all went well until Patrick missed his lunch and charged Ignatius Aloysius with its abstraction. Words ensued which were not easily to be forgotten even when the refreshment was found - flat and horribly distorted - under the portly frame of the chaperon.

Jealousy may have played some part in the misunderstanding, for it was undeniable that there was a sprightliness, a joyant brightness, in the flowing red scarf on Ignatius Aloysius's nautical breast, which was nowhere paralleled in Patrick's more subdued array. And the tenth commandment seemed very arbitrary to Patrick, the star of St. Mary's Sunday-school, when he saw that the red silk was attracting nearly all the attention of his female contingent. If Eva admired flaunting ties it were well that she should say so now. There was yet time to spare himself the agony of riding on rubber-neck-boat-birds with one whose interest wandered from brass buttons. Darkly Patrick scowled upon his unconscious rival, and guilefully he remarked to Eva:

"Red neckties is nice, don't you think?"

"Awful nice," Eva agreed; "but they ain't so stylish like

high-stiffs. High-stiffs und derbies is awful stylish."

Gloom and darkness vanished from the heart and countenance of the Knight of Munster, for around his neck he wore, with suppressed agony, the highest and stiffest of "high-stiffs," and his brows - and the back of his neck - were encircled by his big brother's work-a-day derby. Again he saw and described to Eva the vision which had lived in his hopes for now so many weeks: against a background of teeming jungle, mysterious and alive with wild beasts, an amiable boat-bird floated on the water-lake; and upon the boat-bird, trembling but reassured, sat Eva Gonorowsky, hand in hand with her brass-buttoned protector.

As the car sped up the Bowery the children felt that they were indeed adventurers. The clattering Elevated trains overhead, the crowds of brightly decked Sunday strollers, the clanging trolley cars, and the glimpses they caught of shining green as they passed the streets leading to the smaller squares and parks, all contributed to the holiday upliftedness which swelled their unaccustomed hearts. At each vista of green they made ready to disembark and were restrained only by the conductor and by the sage counsel of Eva, who reminded her impulsive companions that the Central Park could be readily identified by "the hollers from all them things what hollers." And so, in happy watching and calm trust of the conductor, they were borne far beyond 59th Street, the first and most popular entrance to the park, before an interested passenger came to their rescue. They tumbled off the car and pressed towards the green only to find themselves shut out by a high stone wall, against which they crouched and listened in vain for identifying hollers. The silence began to frighten them, when suddenly the quiet air was shattered by a shriek which would have done credit to the biggest of boat-birds or of lions, but which was - the children discovered after a moment's panic - only the prelude to an outburst of grief on the chaperon's part. When the inarticulate stage of her sorrow was passed, she demanded instant speech with her mamma. She would seem to have expressed a sentiment common to the majority, for three heads in Spring finery leaned dejectedly against the stone barrier while Nathan removed his car-fare to contribute the remark that he was growing hungry. Patrick was forced to seek aid in the passing crowd on Fifth Avenue, and in response to his pleading eyes and the depression of his party, a lady of gentle aspect and "kind looks" stopped and spoke to them.

"Indeed, yes," she reassured them; "this is Central Park."

"It has looks off the country," Eva commented.

"Because it is a piece of the country," the lady explained.

"Then we dassent to go, the while we ain't none of us got no sickness," cried Eva forlornly. "We're all, all healthy, und the country is for sick childrens."

"I am glad you are well," said the lady kindly; "but you may certainly play in the park. It is meant for all little children. The gate is near. Just walk on near this wall until you come to it."

It was only a few blocks, and they were soon in the land of their hearts' desire, where were waving trees and flowering shrubs and smoothly sloping lawns, and, framed in all these wonders, a beautiful little water-lake all dotted and brightened by fleets of tiny boats. The pilgrims from the East Side stood for a moment at gaze and then bore down upon the jewel, straight over grass and border, which is a course not lightly to be followed in park precincts and in view of park policemen. The ensuing reprimand dashed their spirits not at all and they were soon assembled close to the margin of the lake, where they got entangled in guiding strings and drew to shore many a craft, to the disgust of many a small owner. Becky Zalmonowsky stood so closely over the lake that she shed the chatelaine bag into its shallow depths and did irreparable damage to her gala costume in her attempts to "dibble" for her property. It was at last recovered, no wetter than the toilette it was intended to adorn, and the cousins Gonorowsky had much difficulty in balking Becky's determination to remove her gown and dry it then and there.

Then Ignatius Aloysius, the exacting, remembered garrulously that he had as yet seen nothing of the rubber-neck-boat-birds and suggested that they were even now graciously "hollering like an'thing" in some remote fastness of the park. So Patrick gave commands and the march was resumed with bliss now beaming on all the faces so lately clouded. Every turn of the endless walks brought new wonders to these little ones who were gazing for the first time upon the great world of growing things of which Miss Bailey had so often told them. The policeman's warning had been explicit and they followed decorously in the paths and picked none of the flowers which, as Eva had heard of old, were sticking right up out of the ground. And other flowers there were dangling high or low on tree or shrub, while here and there across the grass a bird came hopping or a squirrel ran. But the pilgrims never swerved. Full well they knew that these delights were not for such as they.

It was, therefore, with surprise and concern that they at last debouched upon a wide green space where a flag waved at the top of a towering pole; for, behold, the grass was covered thick with children, with here and there a beneficent policeman looking serenely on.

"Dast *we* walk on it?" cried Morris. "Oh, Patrick, dast we?"

"Ask the cop," Nathan suggested. It was his first speech for an hour, for Becky's misadventure with the chatelaine bag and the water-lake had made him more than ever sure that his own method of safe-keeping was the best.

"Ask him yerself," retorted Patrick. He had quite intended to accost a large policeman, who would of course recognize and revere the buttons of Mr. Brennan *pere*, but a commander cannot well accept the advice of his subordinates. But Nathan was once more beyond the power of speech, and it was Morris Mogilewsky who asked for and obtained permission to walk on God's green earth. With little spurts of running and tentative jumps to test its spring, they crossed Peacock Lawn to the grateful shade of the trees at its further edge and there disposed themselves upon the ground and ate their luncheon. Nathan Spiderwitz waited until Sadie had finished and then entrusted the five gleaming pennies to her care while he wildly bolted an appetizing combination of dark brown-bread and uncooked salmon.

Becky reposed upon the chatelaine bag and waved her still damp shoes exultantly. Eva lay, face downward beside her, and peered wonderingly deep into the roots of things.

"Don't it smells nice!" she gloated. "Don't it looks nice! My, ain't we havin' the party-time!"

"Don't mention it," said Patrick, in careful imitation of his mother's hostess's manner. "I'm pleased to see you, I'm sure."

"The Central Park is awful pretty," Sadie soliloquized as she lay on her back and watched the waving branches and blue sky far above. "Awful pretty! I likes we should live here all the time."

"Well," began Ignatius Aloysius Diamantstein, in slight disparagement of his rival's powers as a cicerone; "well, I ain't seen no lions, nor no rubber-neck-boat-birds. Und we ain't had no rides on nothings. Und I ain't heard no hollers neither."

As if in answer to this criticism there arose upon the road beyond the trees a snorting, panting noise, growing momentarily louder and culminating just as East Side nerves were strained to breaking point, in a long, hoarse and terrifying yell. There was a flash of red, a cloud of dust, three other toots of agony, and the thing was gone. Gone, too, were the explorers and gone their peaceful rest. To the distant end of the field they flew, led by the panic-stricken chaperon, and followed by Eva and Patrick, hand in hand, he making show of a bravery he was far from feeling, and she frankly terrified. In a secluded corner, near the restaurant, the chaperon was run to earth by her breathless charges.

"I seen the lion," she panted over and over. "I seen the fierce, big red lion, und I don't know where is my mamma."

Patrick saw that one of the attractions had failed to attract, so he tried another.

"Let's go and see the cows," he proposed. "Don't you know the po'try piece Miss Bailey learned us about cows?"

Again the emotional chaperon interrupted. "I'm loving much mit Miss Bailey, too," she wailed. "Und I don't know where is she neither." But the pride of learning upheld the others and they chanted in singsong chorus, swaying rhythmically the while from leg to leg:

> *"The friendly cow all red and white,*
> *I love with all my heart:*
> *She gives me cream with all her might,*
> *To eat with apple-tart Robert Louis Stevenson."*

Becky's tears ceased. "Be there cows in the Central Park?" she demanded.

"Sure," said Patrick.

"Und what kind from cream will he give us? Ice cream?"

"Sure," said Patrick again.

"Let's go," cried the emotional chaperon. A passing stranger turned the band in the general direction of the menagerie and the reality of the cow brought the whole "memory gem" into strange and undreamed reality.

Gaily they set out through new and always beautiful ways; through tunnels where feet and voices rang with ghostly boomings most pleasant to the ear; over bridges whence they saw - in partial proof of Isaac Borrachsohn's veracity - "mans und ladies ridin'." Of a surety they rode nothing more exciting than horses, but that was, to East Side eyes, an unaccustomed sight, and Eva opined that it was owing, probably, to the shortness of their watch that they saw no lions and tigers similarly amiable. The cows, too, seemed far to seek, but the trees and grass and flowers were everywhere. Through long stretches of "for sure country" they picked their way, until they came, hot but happy, to a green and shady summer house on a hill. There they halted to rest, and there Ignatius Aloysius, with questionable delicacy, began to insist once more upon the full measure of his bond.

"We ain't seen the rubber-neck-boat-birds," he complained. "Und we ain't had no rides on nothings."

"You don't know what is polite," cried Eva, greatly shocked at his carping spirit in the presence of a hard-worked host. "You could to think shame over how you says somethings like that on a party."

"This ain't no party," Ignatius Aloysius retorted. "It's a 'scursion. To a party somebody *gives* you what you should eat; to a 'scursion you *brings* it. Und, anyway, we ain't had no rides."

"But we heard a holler," the guest of honour reminded him. "We heard a fierce, big holler from a lion. I don't know do I need a ride on something what hollers. I could to have a fraid maybe."

"Ye wouldn't be afraid on the boats when I hold yer hand, would ye?" Patrick anxiously inquired, and Eva shyly admitted that, thus supported, she might be undismayed. To work off the pride and joy caused by this avowal, Patrick mounted the broad seat extending all around the summer-house and began to walk clatteringly upon it. The other pilgrims followed suit and the whole party stamped and danced with infinite enjoyment. Suddenly the leader halted with a cry of triumph and pointed grandly out through one of the wistaria-hung openings. Not De Soto upon the banks of the Mississippi nor Balboa above the Pacific could have felt more victorious than Patrick did as he announced:

"There's the water-lake!"

His followers closed in upon him so impetuously that he was borne down under their charge and fell ignominiously out upon the grass. But he was hardly missed; he had served his purpose. For there, beyond the rocks and lawns and red japonicas, lay the blue and shining water-lake in its confining banks of green. And upon its softly quivering surface floated the rubber-neck-boat-birds, white and sweetly silent instead of red and screaming - and the superlative length and arched beauty of their necks surpassed the wildest of Ikey Borrachsohn's descriptions. And relying upon the strength and politeness of these wondrous birds there were indeed "mans und ladies und boys und little girls" embarking, disembarking, and placidly weaving in and out and round about through scenes of hidden but undoubted beauty.

Over rocks and grass the army charged towards bliss unutterable, strewing their path with overturned and howling babies of prosperity who, clumsy from many nurses and much pampering, failed to make way. Past all barriers, accident or official, they pressed, nor halted to draw rein or breath until they were established, beatified, upon the waiting swan-boat.

Three minutes later they were standing outside the railings of the landing and regarding, through welling tears, the placid lake, the sunny slopes of grass and tree, the brilliant sky and the gleaming rubber-neck-boat-bird which, as Ikey described, "made go its legs," but only, as he had omitted to mention, for money. So there they stood, seven sorrowful little figures engulfed in the rayless despair of childhood and the bitterness of poverty. For these were the children of the poor, and full well they knew that money was not to be diverted from its mission: that car-fare could not be squandered on bliss.

Becky's woe was so strong and loud that the bitter wailings of the others served merely as its background. But Patrick cared not at all for the general despair. His remorseful eyes never strayed from the bowed figure of Eva Gonorowsky, for whose pleasure and honour he had striven so long and vainly. Slowly she conquered her sobs, slowly she raised her daisy-decked head, deliberately she blew her small pink nose, softly she approached her conquered knight, gently and all untruthfully she faltered, with yearning eyes on the majestic swans: "Don't you have no sad feelings, Patrick. I ain't got none. Ain't I told you from long, how I don't need no rubber-neck-boat-bird rides? I don't need 'em! I don't need em! I" - with a sob of passionate longing - "I'm got all times a awful scare over 'em. Let's go home, Patrick. Becky needs she should see her mamma, und I guess I needs my mamma too."

A PASSPORT TO PARADISE

School had been for some months in progress when the footsteps of Yetta Aaronsohn were turned, by a long-suffering Truant Officer, in the direction of Room 18. During her first few hours among its pictures, plants and children, she sadly realized the great and many barriers which separated her from Eva Gonorowsky, Morris Mogilewsky, Patrick Brennan, and other favoured spirits who basked in the sunshine of Teacher's regard. For, with a face too white, hair too straight, dresses too short and legs too long one runs a poor chance in rivalry with more blessed and bedizened children.

Miss Bailey had already appointed her monitors, organized her kingdom, and was so hedged about with servitors and assistants that her wishes were acted upon before a stranger could surmise them, and her Cabinet, from the Leader of the Line to the Monitor of the Gold-Fish Bowl, presented an impregnable front to the aspiring public.

During recess time Yetta learned that Teacher was further entrenched in groundless prejudice. Sarah Schrodsky, class bureau of etiquette and of *savoir faire*, warned the new-comer:

"Sooner you comes on the school mit dirt on the face

she wouldn't to have no kind feelin's over you. She don't lets you should set by her side: she don't lets you should be monitors off of somethings: she don't lets you should make an'thing what is nice fer you."

Another peculiarity was announced by Sadie Gonorowsky: "So you comes late on the school, she has fierce mads. Patrick Brennan, he comes late over yesterday on the morning und she don't lets he should march first on the line."

"Did she holler?" asked Yetta, in an awed whisper.

"No. She don't need she should holler when she has mads. She looks on you mit long-mad-proud-looks und you don't needs no hollers. She could to have mads 'out sayin' nothings und you could to have a scare over it. It's fierce. Und extra she goes und tells it out to Patrick's papa - he's the cop mit buttons what stands by the corner - how Patrick comes late und Patrick gets killed as anything over it."

"On'y Patrick ain't cried," interrupted Eva Gonorowsky. She had heard her hero's name and sprang to his defence. "Patrick tells me how his papa hits him awful hacks mit a club. I don't know what is a club, on'y Patrick says it makes him biles on all his bones."

"You gets biles on your bones from off of cops sooner you comes late on the school!" gasped Yetta. "Nobody ain't tell me nothings over that. I don't know, neither, what is clubs - "

"I know what they are," the more learned Sarah Schrodsky began. "It's a house mit man's faces in the windows. It's full from mans by night. Ikey Borrachsohn's papa's got one mit music inside."

"I don't likes it! I have a fraid over it!" wailed Yetta. "I don't know does my mamma likes I should come somewheres where cops mit buttons makes like that mit me. I don't know is it healthy fer me."

"Sooner you don't comes late on the school nobody makes like that mit you," Eva reminded the panic-stricken new-comer, and for the first three days of her school life Yetta was very early and very dirty.

Miss Bailey, with gentle tact, delivered little lectures upon the use and beauty of soap and water which Eva Gonorowsky applied to and discussed with the new-comer.

"Miss Bailey is a awful nice Teacher," she began one afternoon. "I never in my world seen no nicer teacher. On'y she's fancy."

"I seen how she's fancy," Yetta agreed. "She's got her hair done fancy mit combs und her waist is from fancy goods."

"Yes, she's fancy," Eva continued. "She likes you should put you on awful clean. Say, what you think, she sends a boy home once - mit notes even - the while he puts him on mit dirty sweaters. She says like this: 'Sweaters what you wears by nights und by days ain't stylish fer school.' Und I guess she knows what is stylish. I ain't never in my world seen no stylisher teacher."

"I don't know be buttoned-in-back dresses the style this

year," ventured Yetta. The same misgiving had visited Eva, but she thrust it loyally from her.

"They're the latest," she declared.

"It's good they're the style," sighed Yetta. "Mine dress is a buttoned-in-back-dress, too. On'y I loses me the buttons from off of it. I guess maybe I sews 'em on again. Teacher could to have, maybe, kind feelings, sooner she sees how I puts me on mit buttons on mine back und - "

"Sure could she!" interrupted the sustaining Eva.

"Could she have kind feelings sooner I puts me on clean mit buttons on mine back und makes all things what is nice fer me? Oh, Eva, could she have feelin's over me?"

"Sure could she," cried Eva. "Sooner you makes all them things she could to make you, maybe, monitors off of somethings."

"Be you monitors?" demanded Yetta in sudden awe.

"Off of pencils. Ain't you seen how I gives 'em out and takes 'em up? She gives me too a piece of paper mit writings on it. Sooner I shows it on the big boys what stands by the door in the yard, sooner they lets me I should come right up by Teacher's room. You could to look on it." And, after unfolding countless layers of paper and of cheese-cloth handkerchief, she exhibited her talisman. It was an ordinary visiting card with a line of writing under its neatly engraved "Miss Constance Bailey," and Yetta regarded it with envying eyes. "What does it says?" she asked.

"Well," admitted Eva with reluctant candour, "I couldn't to read them words but I guess it says I should come all places what I wants the while I'm good girls."

"Can you go all places where you wants mit it?"

"Sure could you."

"On theaytres?"

"Sure."

"On the Central Park?"

"Sure."

"On the country? Oh I guess you couldn't to go on the country mit it?"

"Sure could you. All places what you wants you could to go sooner Missis Bailey writes on papers how you is good girls."

"Oh, how I likes she should write like that fer me. Oh, how I likes I should be monitors off of somethings."

"I tell you what you want to do: wash your hands!" cried Eva, with sudden inspiration. "She's crazy for what is clean. You wash your hands und your face. She could to have feelin's."

For some mornings thereafter Yetta was clean - and late. Miss Bailey overlooked the cleanliness, but noted the tardiness, and treated the offender with some of "the mads 'out sayin' nothings" which Sadie had predicted. Still, the "cop mit buttons und clubs" did not appear, though Yetta lived in constant terror and expected that every opening of the door would disclose that dread avenger.

On the fourth morning of her ablutions Yetta reached Room 18 while a reading lesson was absorbing Teacher's attention:

"Powers above!" ejaculated Patrick Brennan, with all the ostentatious virtue of the recently reformed, "here's that new kid late again!"

The new kid, in copious tears, encountered one of the "long-mad-proud-looks" and cringed.

"Why are you late?" demanded Miss Bailey.

"I washes me the face," whimpered the culprit, and the eyes with which she regarded Eva Gonorowsky added tearfully: "Villain behold your work!"

"So I see, but that is no reason for being late. You have been late twice a day, morning and afternoon, for the last three days and your only excuse has been that you were washing your face. Which is no excuse at all."

"I tells you 'scuse," pleaded Yetta. "I tells you 'scuse."

"Very well, I'll forgive you to-day. I suppose I must tolerate you."

"No-o-oh ma'an, Teacher, Missis Bailey, don't you do it," screamed Yetta in sudden terror. "I'd have a awful frightened over it. I swear, I kiss up to God, I wouldn't never no more come late on the school. I don't needs nobody should make nothings like that mit me."

"Oh, it's not so bad," Miss Bailey reassured her. "And you must expect something to happen if you *will* come late to school for no reason at all."

And Yetta was too disturbed by the danger so narrowly escaped to tell this charming but most strangely ignorant young person that the washing of a face was a most time-consuming process. Yetta's one-roomed home was on the top floor, the sixth, and the only water supply was in the yard. Since the day her father had packed "assorted notions" into a black and shiny box and had set out to seek his very elusive fortunes in the country, Yetta had toiled three times a morning with a tin pail full of water. This formed the family's daily store and there was no surplus to be squandered. But to win Teacher's commendation she had bent her tired energies to another trip and, behold, her reward was a scolding!

Eva Gonorowsky was terribly distressed, and the plaintive sobs which, from time to time, rent the bosom of Yetta's dingy plaid dress were as so many blows upon her adviser's bruised conscience. Desperately she cast about for some device by which Teacher's favour might be reclaimed and all jubilantly she imparted it to Yetta.

"Say," she whispered, "I tell you what you want to do. You leave your mamma wash your dress."

"I don't know would she like it. I washes me the face fer her und she has a mad on me."

"She'd like it, all right, all right; ain't I tell you how she is crazy fer what is clean? You get your dress washed and it will look awful diff'rent. I done it und she had a glad."

Now a mamma who supports a family by the making of buttonholes, for one hundred of which she receives nine cents, has little time for washing, and Yetta determined, unaided and unadvised, to be her own laundress. She made endless trips with her tin-pail from the sixth floor to the yard and back again, she begged a piece of soap from the friendly "janitor lady" and set valiantly to work. And Eva's prophecy was fulfilled. The dress looked "awful diff'rent" when it had dried to half its already scant proportions. From various sources Yetta collected six buttons of widely dissimilar design and colour and, with great difficulty since her hands were puffed and clumsy from long immersion in strong suds, she affixed them to the back of the dress and fell into her corner of the family couch to dream of Miss Bailey's surprise and joy when the blended plaid should be revealed unto her. Surely, if there were any gratitude in the hearts of teachers, Yetta should be, ere the sinking of another sun, "monitors off of somethings."

That Teacher was surprised, no one who saw the glance of puzzled inquiry with which she greeted the entrance of the transformed Yetta, could doubt. That she had a glad, Yetta, who saw the stare replaced by a smile of quick recognition, was proudly assured. Eva Gonorowsky shone triumphant.

"Ain't I tell you?" she whispered jubilantly as she made room upon her little bench and drew Yetta down beside her. "Ain't I tell you how she's crazy fer what is clean? Und I ain't never seen nothings what is clean like you be. You smells off of soap even."

It was not surprising, for Yetta had omitted the rinsing which some laundresses advise. She had wasted none of the janitor lady's gift. It was all in the meshes of the flannel dress to which it lent, in addition to its reassuring perfume, a smooth damp slipperiness most pleasing to the touch.

The athletic members of the First Reader Class were made familiar with this quality before the day was over, for, at the slightest exertion of its wearer, the rain-bow dress sprang, chrysalis-like, widely open up the back. Then were the combined efforts of two of the strongest members of the class required to drag the edges into apposition while Eva guided the buttons to their respective holes and Yetta "let go of her breath" with an energy which defeated its purpose.

These interruptions of the class routine were so inevitable a consequence of Swedish exercises and gymnastics that Miss Bailey was forced to sacrifice Yetta's physical development to the general discipline and to anchor her in quiet waters during the frequent periods of drill. When she had been in time she sat at Teacher's desk in a glow of love and pride. When she had been late she stood in a corner near the book-case and repented of her sin. And, despite all her exertions and Eva's promptings, she was still occasionally late.

Miss Bailey was seriously at a loss for some method of dealing with a child so wistful of eyes and so damaging of habits. A teacher's standing on the books of the Board of Education depends to a degree upon the punctuality and regularity of attendance to which she can inspire her class, and Yetta was reducing the average to untold depths.

"What happened to-day?" Teacher asked one morning for the third time in one week, and through Yetta's noisy repentance she heard hints of "store" and "mamma."

"Your mamma sent you to the store?" she interpreted and Yetta nodded dolefully.

"And did you give her my message about that last week? Did you tell her that she *must* send you to school before nine o'clock?" Again Yetta nodded, silent and resigned, evidently a creature bound upon the wheel, heart broken but uncomplaining.

"Well, then," began Miss Bailey, struggling to maintain her just resentment, "you can tell her now that I want to see her. Ask her to come to school to-morrow morning."

"Teacher, she couldn't. She ain't got time. Und she don't know where is the school neither."

"That's nonsense. You live only two blocks away. She sees it every time she passes the corner."

"She don't never pass no corner. She don't never come on the street. My mamma ain't got time. She sews."

"But she can't sew always. She goes out, doesn't she, to do shopping and to see her friends?"

"She ain't got friends. She ain't got time she should have 'em. She sews all times. Sooner I lays me und the babies on the bed by night my mamma sews. Und sooner I stands up in mornings my mamma sews. All, *all*, ALL times she sews."

"And where is your father? Doesn't he help?"

"Teacher, he's on the country. He is pedlar mans. He walk und he walk und he walk mit all things what is stylish in a box. On'y nobody wants they should buy somethings from off of my papa. No ma'an, Missis Bailey, that ain't how they makes mit my poor papa. They goes und makes dogs should bite him on the legs. That's how he tells in a letter what he writes on my mamma. Comes no money in the letter und me und my mamma we got it pretty hard. We got three babies."

"I'm going home with you this afternoon," announced Miss Bailey in a voice which suggested neither mads nor clubs nor violence.

After that visit things were a shade more bearable in the home of the absent pedlar, and one-half of Yetta's ambition was achieved. Teacher had a glad! There was a gentleness almost apologetic in her attitude and the hour after which an arrival should be met with a long-proud-mad-look was indefinitely postponed. And, friendly relations being established, Yetta's craving for monitorship grew with the passing days.

When she expressed to Teacher her willingness to hold office she was met with unsatisfying but baffling generalities.

"But surely I shall let you be monitor some day. I have monitors for nearly everything under the sun, now, but perhaps I shall think of something for you."

"I likes," faltered Yetta; "I likes I should be monitor off of flowers." "But Nathan Spiderwitz takes care of the window boxes. He won't let even me touch them.

Think what he would do to you."

"Then I likes I should be monitors to set by your place when you goes by the Principal's office."

"But Patrick Brennan always takes care of the children when I am not in the room."

"He marches first by the line too. He's two monitors."

"He truly is," agreed Miss Bailey. "Well, I shall let you try that some day."

It was a most disastrous experiment. The First Reader Class, serenely good under the eye of Patrick Brennan, who wore one of the discarded brass buttons of his sire pinned to the breast of his shirt-waist, found nothing to fear or to obey in his supplanter, and Miss Bailey returned to her kingdom to find it in an uproar and her regent in tears.

"I don't likes it. I don't likes it," Yetta wailed. "All the boys shows a fist on me. All the girls makes a snoot on me. All the childrens say cheek on me. I don't likes it. I don't likes it."

"Then you sha'n't do it again," Teacher comforted her. "You needn't be a monitor if you don't wish."

"But I likes I shall be monitors. On'y not that kind from monitors."

"If you can think of something you would enjoy I shall let you try again. But it must be something, dear, that no one is doing for me."

But Yetta could think of nothing until one afternoon when she was sitting at Teacher's desk during a Swedish drill. All about her were Teacher's things. Her large green blotter, her "from gold" inkstand and pens, her books where Fairies lived. Miss Bailey was standing directly in front of the desk and encouraging the First Reader Class - by command and example - to strenuous waving of arms and bending of bodies.

"Forward bend!" commanded, and bent, Miss Bailey and her buttoned-in-back-waist followed the example of less fashionable models, shed its pearl buttons in a shower upon the smooth blotter and gave Yetta the inspiration for which she had been waiting. She gathered the buttons, extracted numerous pins from posts of trust in her attire, and when Miss Bailey had returned to her chair, gently set about repairing the breach.

"What is it?" asked Miss Bailey. Yetta, her mouth full of pins, exhibited the buttons.

"Dear me! All those off!" exclaimed Teacher. "It was good of you to arrange it for me. And now will you watch it? You'll tell me if it should open again?"

Yetta had then disposed the pins to the best advantage and was free to voice her triumphant:

"Oh, I knows *now* how I wants I should be monitors! Teacher, mine dear Teacher, could I be monitors off of the back of your dress?"

"But surely, you may," laughed Teacher, and Yetta entered straightway into the heaven of fulfilled desire.

None of Eva's descriptions of the joys of monitorship had done justice to the glad reality. After common mortals had gone home at three o'clock, Room 18 was transformed into a land where only monitors and love abounded. And the new monitor was welcomed by the existing staff, for she had supplanted no one, and was so palpitatingly happy that Patrick Brennan forgave her earlier usurpation of his office and Nathan Spiderwitz bestowed upon her the freedom of the window boxes.

"Ever when you likes you should have a crawley bug from off of the flowers; you tell me und I'll catch one fer you. I got lots. I don't need 'em all."

"I likes I shall have one now," ventured Yetta, and Nathan ensnared one and put it in her hand where it "crawlied" most pleasingly until Morris Mogilewsky begged it for his Gold-Fish in their gleaming "fish theaytre." Then Eva shared with her friend and protege the delight of sharpening countless blunted and bitten pencils upon a piece of sand-paper.

"Say," whispered Yetta as they worked busily and dirtily, "Say, I'm monitors now. On'y I ain't got no papers."

"You ask her. She'll give you one."

"I'd have a shamed the while she gives me und my mamma whole bunches of things already. She could to think, maybe, I'm a greedy. But I needs that paper awful much. I needs I shall go on the country for see mine papa."

"No, she don't thinks you is greedy. Ain't you monitors on the back of her waist? You should come up here 'fore the childrens comes for see how her buttons stands. You go und tell her you needs that paper."

Very diplomatically Yetta did. "Teacher," she began, "buttoned-in-back-dresses is stylish fer ladies."

"Yes, honey," Miss Bailey acquiesced, "so I thought when I saw that you wear one."

"On'y they opens," Yetta went on, all flushed by this high tribute to her correctness. "All times they opens, yours und mine, und that makes us shamed feelings."

Again Miss Bailey acquiesced.

"So-o-oh," pursued Yetta, with fast beating heart; "don't you wants you should give me somethings from paper mit writings on it so I could come on your room all times for see how is your buttoned-in-back-dresses?"

"A beautiful idea," cried Teacher. "We'll take care of one another's buttons. I'll write the card for you now. You know what to do with it?"

"Yiss ma'an. Eva tells me all times how I could come where I wants sooner you writes on papers how I is good girls."

"I'll write nicer things than that on yours," said Miss Bailey. "You are one of the best little girls in the world. So useful to your mother and to the babies and to me! Oh yes, I'll write beautiful things on your card, my dear."

When the Grand Street car had borne Miss Bailey

away Yetta turned to Eva with determination in her eye and the "paper mit writings" in her hand.

"I'm goin' on the country for see my papa und birds und flowers und all them things what Teacher tells stands in the country. I need I should see them."

"Out your mamma?" Eva remonstrated.

"'Out, 'out my mamma. She ain't got no time for go on no country. I don't needs my mamma should go by my side. Ain't you said I could to go all places what I wants I should go, sooner Teacher gives me papers mit writings?"

"Sure could you," Eva repeated solemnly. "There ain't no place where you couldn't to go mit it."

"I'll go on the country," said Yetta.

That evening Mrs. Aaronsohn joined her neighbours upon the doorstep for the first time in seven years. For Yetta was lost. The neighbours were comforting but not resourceful. They all knew Yetta; knew her to be sensible and mature for her years even according to the exacting standard of the East Side. She would presently return, they assured the distraught Mrs. Aaronsohn, and pending that happy event they entertained her with details of the wanderings and home comings of their own offspring. But Yetta did not come. The reminiscent mothers talked themselves into silence, the deserted babies cried themselves to sleep. Mrs. Aaronsohn carried them up to bed - she hardly knew the outer aspect of her own door - and returned to the then deserted doorstep to watch for her first-born. One by one the lights were extinguished, the sewing-machines stopped, and the restless night of the quarter closed down. She was afraid to go even as far as the corner in search of the fugitive. She could not have recognized the house which held her home.

All her hopes were centered in the coming of Miss Bailey. When the children of happier women were setting out for school she demanded and obtained from one of them safe conduct to Room 18. But Teacher, when Eva Gonorowsky had interpreted the tale of Yetta's disappearance, could suggest no explanation.

"She was with me until half-past three. Then she and Eva walked with me to the corner. Did she tell you, dear, where she was going?"

"Teacher, yiss ma'an. She says she goes on the country for see her papa und birds und flowers."

When this was put into Jewish for Mrs. Aaronsohn she was neither comforted nor reassured. Miss Bailey was puzzled but undismayed. "We'll find her," she promised the now tearful mother. "I shall go with you to look for her. Say that in Jewish for me, Eva."

The Principal lent a substitute. Room 18 was deserted by its sovereign: the pencils were deserted by their monitor: and Mrs. Aaronsohn, Miss Bailey and Eva Gonorowsky, official interpreter, set out for the nearest drug-store where a telephone might be. They inspected several unclaimed children before, in the station of a precinct many weary blocks away, they came upon Yetta. She was more dirty and bedraggled than she had ever been, but the charm of her manner was unchanged and, suspended about her neck, she wore a policeman's button.

"One of the men brought her in here at ten o'clock last night," the man behind the blotter informed Miss Bailey, while Mrs. Aaronsohn showered abuse and caress upon the wanderer. "She was straying around the Bowery and she gave us a great game of talk about her father bein' a bird. I guess he is."

"My papa und birds is on the country. I likes I shall go there," said Yetta from the depths of her mother's embrace.

"There, that's what she tells everyone. She has a card there with a Christian name and no address on it. I was going to try to identify her by looking for this Miss Constance Bailey."

"That is my name. I am her teacher. I gave her the card because - "

"I'm monitors. I should go all places what I wants the while I'm good girls und Teacher writes it on pieces from paper. On'y I ain't want I should come on no cops' house. I likes I should go on the country for see my papa und birds und flowers. I says like that on a cop - I shows him the paper even - und he makes I shall come here on the cops' house where my papa don't stands und birds don't stands und flowers don't stands."

"When next you want to go to the country," said Teacher, "you ought to let us know. You have frightened us all dreadfully and that is a very naughty thing to do. If you ever run away again I shall have to keep the promise I made to you long and long ago when you used to come late to school. I shall have to tolerate you."

But Yetta was undismayed. "I ain't got no more a scare over that," said she with a soft smile towards the brass-buttoned person behind the blotter. "Und I ain't got no scare over cops neither; I never in mine world seen how they makes all things what is polite mit me und gives me I should eat."

"Well," cautioned Teacher "you must never do it again," and turned her attention to the very erratic spelling of Sergeant Moloney's official record of the flight of Yetta Aaronsohn.

"Say," whispered Eva, and there was a tinge of jealousy in her soft voice; "say, who gives you the button like Patrick Brennan's got?"

"THE COP," answered Yetta, pointing a dirty but reverential finger towards her new divinity. "I guess maybe I turns me the dress around. Buttoned-in-front-mit-from-gold-button-suits is awful stylish. He's got 'em."

"Think shame how you says," cried Eva, with loyal eyes upon the neatly buttoned and all unsuspecting back of Miss Bailey, "Ain't you seen how is Teacher's back?"

"Ain't I monitors off of it?" demanded Yetta. "Sure I know how is it. On'y I don't know be they so stylish. Cops ain't got 'em und, oh Eva, Cops is somethin' grand! I turns me the dress around."

THE TOUCH OF NATURE

"There is," wrote the authorities with a rare enthusiasm, "no greater power for the mental, moral and physical uplifting of the Child than a knowledge and an appreciation of the Beauties of Nature. It is the duty and the privilege of the teacher to bring this elevating influence into the lives of the children for whom she is responsible." There are not many of the Beauties of Nature to be found on the lower East Side of New York, and Miss Bailey found this portion of her duty full of difficulty. Excursions were out of the question, and she discovered that specimens conveyed but crudely erroneous ideas to the minds of her little people. She was growing discouraged at the halting progress of the First Reader Class in Natural Science, when, early in October, the Principal ushered into Room 18, Miss Eudora Langdon, Lecturer on Biology and Nature Study in a Western university, a shining light in the world of education, and an orator in her own conceit.

"I shall leave Miss Langdon with you for a short time, Miss Bailey," said the Principal when the introductions had been accomplished. "She is interested in the questions which are troubling you, and would like to speak to the children if you have no objection."

"Surely none," replied Miss Bailey; and when the

Principal had retired to interview parents and book-agents, she went on: "I find it difficult to make Nature Study real to the children. They regard it all as fairy-lore."

"Ah, yes," the visitor admitted; "it does require some skill. You should appeal to their sense of the beautiful."

"But I greatly fear," said Teacher sadly, "that the poor babies know very little about beauty."

"Then develop the ideal," cried Miss Langdon, and the eyes behind her glasses shone with zeal. "Begin this very day. Should you like me to open up a topic?"

"If you will be so very good," said Teacher, with some covert amusement, and Miss Langdon, laying her notebook on the desk, turned to address the class. Immediately Nathan Spiderwitz, always on the alert for bad news, started a rumour which spread from desk to desk - "Miss Bailey could to be goin' away. This could be a new teacher."

"My dears," Miss Eudora began, with deliberate and heavy coyness; "I'm *so* fond of little children! I've always loved them. That's why your kind Principal brought me here to talk to you. Now, wasn't that good of him?"

At this confirmation of their fears the First Reader Class showed so moderate a joy that Miss Langdon hurried on: "And what would you like me to tell you about?"

"Lions," said Patrick Brennan promptly. "Big hairy

lions with teeth."

The visitor paused almost blankly while the children brightened. Miss Bailey struggled with a rebellious laugh, but Miss Langdon recovered quickly.

"I shall tell you," she began serenely, "about Beauty. Beauty is one of the greatest things in the world. Beauty makes us strong. Beauty makes us happy. I want you all to think - think hard - and tell me what we can do to make our lives more beautiful."

Fifty-eight pairs of troubled eyes sought inspiration in the face of the rightful sovereign. Fifty-eight little minds wrestled dumbly.

"Well, I suppose I must help you," said Miss Eudora with elephantine sprightliness. "Now, children, in the first place you must always read beautiful books; then, always look at beautiful things; and lastly, always think beautiful thoughts."

"Miss Langdon," Teacher gently interposed, "these children cannot read very much - twenty-five words perhaps - and for the majority of them, poor little things, this school-room is the prettiest place in the world."

"Oh, that's all right. My text is right there," said the visitor, with a nod towards a tree, the only large one in the district, which was visible through the window. It had not yet lost its leaves, and a shower during the preceding night had left it passably green. Turning to the children, now puzzled into fretful unhappiness, she clasped her hands, closed her eyes in rapture, and proceeded:

"You all know how Beauty helps you. How it strengthens you for your work. Why, in the morning when you come to school you see a beautiful thing which cheers you for the whole day. Now, see if you can't tell me what it is."

Another heavy silence followed and Miss Langdon turned again to Teacher.

"Don't you teach them by the Socratic method?" she asked loftily.

"Oh, yes," Miss Bailey replied, and then, with a hospitable desire to make her guest feel quite at home, she added: "But facts must be closely correlated with their thought-content. Their apperceiving basis is not large."

"Ah, yes; of course," said the expert vaguely, but with a new consideration, and then to the waiting class: "Children, the beautiful thing I'm thinking of is green. Can't you think of something green and beautiful which you see every morning?"

Eva Gonorowsky's big brown eyes fixed solemnly upon Teacher, flamed with sudden inspiration, and Teacher stiffened with an equally sudden fear. For smoothly starched and green was her whole shirtwaist, and carefully tied and green was her neat stock.

Eva whispered jubilantly to Morris Mogilewsky, and another rumour swept the ranks. Intelligence flashed into face after face, and Miss Bailey knew that her fear was not unfounded, for, though Miss Langdon was waving an explanatory arm towards the open window, the gaze of the First Reader Class, bright with appreciation and amusement, was fixed on its now distracted teacher.

"You can see this beautiful green joy sometimes when you are in the street," Miss Langdon ambled on; "but you see it best when you are here."

Three hands shot up into the quiet air.

"And I don't think the children in the other rooms see it as well as you do."

"No ma'am," cried a delighted chorus, and eight more hands were raised. Prompting was reckless now and hands sprang up in all directions.

"No, I don't think they do," Miss Langdon agreed. "I think perhaps that Heaven meant it just for you. Just for the good little boys and girls in this room."

The enthusiasm grew wild and general. Miss Langdon turned a glance of triumph upon Miss Bailey, and was somewhat surprised by the very scarlet confusion which she saw.

"It's all in the method," she said with pride, and, to the class: "Now, can you tell me the name of this beautiful green thing which makes us all so happy?"

And the answer was a great, glad cry of: "Teacher's jumper!"

"What?"

"Teacher's jumper!" shouted the children as before, and Eva Gonorowsky, who had been the first to guess the jocular lady's meaning, put it more plainly.

"Missis Bailey's got a green waist. Green is all the style this year."

Miss Langdon sat down suddenly; stared; gasped; and then, as she was a clever woman, laughed.

"Miss Bailey," she said, "you have a problem here. I wish you all success, but the apperceiving basis is, as you say, very limited."

To the solving of this problem Teacher bent all her energies. Through diligent research she learned that the reading aloud of standard poems has been known to do wonders of mental and moral uplifting. But standard poems are not commonly adapted to minds six years old and of foreign extraction, so that Miss Bailey, though she explained, paraphrased, and commented, hardly flattered herself that the result was satisfactory. In courteous though puzzled silence the First Reader Class listened to enough of the poetry of the ages to have lifted them as high as Heaven. Wordsworth, Longfellow, Browning, any one who had seen and written of the beauty of bird or growing thing, was pressed into service. And then one day Miss Bailey brought her Shelley down and read his "Ode to the Skylark."

"Now, don't you think that's a pretty thing?" she asked. "Did you hear how the lark went singing, bright and clear, up and up and up into the blue sky?"

The children were carefully attentive, as ever, but not responsive. Morris Mogilewsky felt that he had alone understood the nature of this story. It was meant to amuse; therefore it was polite that one should be amused.

"Teacher fools," he chuckled. "Larks ain't singin' in skies."

"How do you know?" asked Miss Bailey.

"'Cause we got a lark by our house. It's a from tin lark mit a cover."

"A tin lark! With a cover!" Miss Bailey exclaimed. "Are you sure, dear, that you know what you are talking about?"

"Teacher, yiss ma'an, I know," Morris began deliberately. "My papa, he has a lark. It's a from tin lark mit a cover. Und its got a handle too. Und my papa he takes it all times on the store for buy a lark of beer."

"Lager beer! Oh, shade of Shelley!" groaned Miss Bailey's spirit, but aloud she only said: "No, my dear, I wasn't reading about lager beer. A lark is a little bird."

"Well," Morris began with renewed confidence, "I know what is a bird. My auntie she had one from long. She says like that, she should give it to me, but my mamma she says, 'No, birds is foolishness.' But I know what is a bird. He scups on a stick in a cage."

"So he does," agreed Miss Bailey, rightly inferring from Morris's expressive pantomime that to "scup" was to swing. "But sometimes he flies up into the sky in the country, as I was reading to you. Were you ever in the country?"

"What country?" asked Morris. "Russia? I comes out of Russia."

"No, not Russia. Not any particular country. Just the open country where the flowers grow."

"No ma'an, I ain't seen it," said the child gently. "But I was once to Tompkins Square. On'y it was winter und snow lays on it. I ain't seen no flowers."

"And do none of you know anything about the country?" asked Teacher sadly.

"Oh, yiss ma'an, I know," said Eva Gonorowsky. "The country is the Fresh Air Fund."

"Then you've been there," cried Miss Bailey. "Tell us about it, Eva."

"No ma'an, I ain't seen it," said Eva proudly. "I'm healthy. But a girl on my block she had a sickness und so she goes. She tells me all times how is the country. It's got grass stickin' right up out of it. Grass und flowers! No ma'an, I ain't never seen it: I don't know where is it even, but oh! it could to be awful pretty!"

"Yes, honey, it is," said Teacher. "Very, very pretty. When I was a little girl I lived in the country."

"All day?" asked Morris.

"Yes, all day."

"Und all night?"

"Yes, dear."

"Oh, poor Miss Bailey," crooned Eva. "It could to be a awful sickness what you had."

"No, I was very well. I lived in the country because my father had a house there, and I played all day in the garden."

"Weren't you scared of the lions?" asked Patrick in incredulous admiration.

"We had no lions," Miss Bailey explained apologetically. "But we had rabbits and guinea pigs and a horse and a cow and chickens and ducks and - and - "

"Und eleflints," Morris suggested hope-fully.

"No, we had no elephants," Teacher was forced to admit. "But we had a turtle and a monkey."

"Did your papa have a organ?" asked Sadie Gonorowsky. "Organs mit monkeys is stylish for mans."

"Think shame how you says!" cried her cousin Eva reproachfully. "Teacher ain't no Ginney. Organs ain't for Sheenies. They ain't for Krishts even. They all, all for Ginneys."

"So's monkeys," said Sadie, unabashed. "Und organs mit monkeys *is* stylish."

The children's deep interest in the animal kingdom gave Miss Bailey the point of departure for which she had been seeking. She abandoned Wordsworth and Shelley, and she bought a rabbit and a pair of white mice. The First Reader Class was enchanted. A canary in a gilded cage soon hung before the window and "scupped" most energetically while gold-fish in their bowl swam lazily back and forth. From these living texts, Miss Bailey easily preached care and kindness towards all creatures, and Room 18 came to be an energetic though independent branch of the S.P.C.A.

The most sincere and zealous worker in the new field was Morris Mogilewsky, Monitor of the Gold-Fish Bowl. Day after day he earned new smiles and commendations from his liege lady by reports of cats and kittens fed and warmed, and of dogs rescued from torment. He was awakened one night by the cries of an outcast cat and followed the sounds to the roof of his tenement only to find that they came from another roof further down the block. The night was wet and blustering, but Morris was undismayed. He crawled over walls and round chimneys until he reached the cat and dragged her back to safety and refreshment. When, in the early dark of the next morning, Mrs. Mogilewsky discovered that the elements of the family breakfast had been lavished on the wanderer, she showed some natural resentment, but when she understood that such prodigally was encouraged, even rewarded, in high places, her wrath was very great.

"So-o-oh, you foolishness like that on the school learns!" she fumed. "Und your teacher she learns you you should like so mil your papa's breakfast und cats make! She is then fine teacher!"

"She's a awful nice teacher," cried Morris, with hot loyalty. "Awful nice. Sooner you seen her sooner you could to be loving mit her too. Ain't you *never* comin' on the school for to see mine teacher?"

"No!" his mother almost shrieked. "No! I seen her on the street once und she had looks off of Krishts. I don't need no Krishts. You don't need them neither. They ain't for us. You ain't so big like I could to tell you how they makes mit us in Russia. I don't like you should hold so much over no Krisht. For us they is devils."

"Teacher ain't no devil," cried Morris, and he would have laid down his loyal life to have been able to add now, as he had some months earlier, "she ain't no Krisht neither," but he knew that his mother had guessed truly. Teacher was a Christian, she had told him so, and he had sworn to protect her secret.

His mother's constant though generally smouldering hostility towards Miss Bailey troubled and puzzled him. In fact, many things were beyond his under-standing. Night after night he lay in his corner behind the stove and listened while his father and his father's friends railed against the Christians and the Czar. He had seen strange meetings of grim and intent men, had listened to low reading of strange threats and mad reviling. And always he gathered that the Christian was a thing unspeakable, unknowable, without truth, or heart or trust. A thing to be feared and hated now but, in the glorious future, when the God of Israel should be once more remindful of his people, a thing to be triumphed over and trampled on.

Yet each morning Morris waited at the big school door for the smile of a lady's face, the touch of a lady's hand, and each day he learned new gentleness and love, new interests and new wonders under her calm-eyed dominion. And behold, the lady was a Christian, and he loved her and she was very good to him!

For his bright service to the cause of Nature in the matter of the cat, she had decorated him, not with a button or a garter - though neither would have been inappropriate - but with a ring bearing his initials gorgeously entwined. Then proud and happy was Morris Mogilewsky, and wild was the emulation of other members of the First Reader Class. Then serious was Teacher's account with a jeweller over in Columbia Street and grave her doubts as to Herr Froebel's blessing on the scheme. But the problem was solved. Of all the busy hours in Room 18's crowded day, there was none more happy than that devoted to "Nature Study - Domestic Animals and Home Pets."

And then one morning Morris failed to answer to the roll-call. Never had he been absent since his first day at school, and Miss Bailey was full of uneasiness. Nathan Spiderwitz, Morris's friend and ally, was also missing, but at half-past nine he arrived entirely breathless and shockingly untidy.

"Nathan," said Teacher reprovingly, "you are very late."

"Yiss ma'an. I tells you 'scuse," gasped Nathan. "On'y Morris - "

"Where is he?" cried Miss Bailey. "Is there anything the matter with him?"

"Yiss ma'an. He ain't got no more that golden ring what you gives him over that cat."

A murmur of commiseration swept through the room. "Oh, poor Morris!" sighed Eva Gonorowsky. "Ain't that fierce! From sure gold rings is awful stylish und they cost whole bunches of money."

"Morris is a silly little boy," said Teacher crossly, for she had been frightened, as it now seemed, to no purpose. "I'll measure his finger for a new ring when he comes in."

"He ain't comin'," said Nathan briefly.

"Not coming to school simply because he lost a ring! Nonsense! Nathan, you just run back to Morris's house and tell him he must come. Tell him I'll give him a new ring and - "

"But he ain't to his house," Nathan objected. "I seen how he goes away."

"Well, then, how did he go away?"

"Teacher, it's like this. Me und Morris we stands by our block when comes the baker's wagon. Und the baker he goes in the groc'ry store to sell bread und his wagon und horse stands by us. Und, say, on the horse's face is something, from leather, so the horse couldn't to eat. He couldn't to open his mouth even. But all times he longs out his neck like he should eat und he looks on me und Morris. So Morris he says: 'Ain't it fierce how that bad man makes mit that horse? Something from leather on the face ain't healthy for horses. I guess I takes it off.'"

"But he didn't, Nathan?"

"Yiss ma'an, he takes it off. He says like that: 'You know how Teacher says we should make all times what is lovin' mit dogs und cats und horses.' Und say,

Teacher, Missis Bailey, that's how you says. He had a ring over it. A from sure gold ring mit his name - "

"But the horse?" Miss Bailey interrupted. "The horse with the muzzle. I remember, dear, what I said, but I hope Morris didn't touch that baker's horse."

"Sure did he," cried Nathan. "He buttons out that thing what I told you from leather, on the horse's face, und the horse he swallows the golden ring."

"Why, I never heard of such a thing," gasped Miss Bailey. And Nathan explained.

"Morris, he gives the horse a sweet potato und the horse he swallows the golden ring. He swallows it way, way, WAY down. Und it was from sure gold-"

"But it must have been very loose or it wouldn't have come off his finger so easily."

"It didn't come off," said Nathan patiently. "The horse he swallowed the finger too - four fingers - und it was from sure gold ring mit his name scratched in on it, what he had off of you, Teacher, for present over that cat."

"Oh, you must be wrong," cried Miss Bailey, "it can't be as bad as you say."

"Yiss ma'an, from sure gold nut - "

"But his hand. Are you sure about his hand?"

"I seen it," said Nathan. "I seen how comes blood on the sidewalk. I seen how comes a great big all of people. I seen how comes Morris's mamma und hollers like a fair theayter. I seen how comes Patrick Brennan's papa - he's a cop - und he makes come the amb'lance. Und sooner the doctor seen how comes blood on the sidewalk he says like this: so Morris bleeds four more inches of blood he don't got no more blood in his body. Say, I seen right into Morris He's red inside. So-o-oh, the doctor he bandages up his hand und takes him in the amb'lance, und all times his mamma hollers und yells und says mad words on the doctor so he had a mad over her. Und Morris he lays in the amb'lance und cries. Now he's sick."

School dragged heavily that morning for the distressed and powerless Miss Bailey. She thought remorsefully of the trusty armour of timidity which she had, plate by plate, stripped from her favourite, and of the bravery and loving kindness which she had so carefully substituted and which had led the child - Where?

"Nathan," she called as the children were going home, "do you know to what hospital Morris was taken? Did you see the doctor?"

"Sure did I."

"Was he a tall doctor? Had you ever seen him before?"

"No ma'an," answered Nathan with a beautiful directness. "It wasn't your fellow We ain't seen him from long. But Morris he goes on the Guv'neer Hospital. I ain't never seen the doctor, but I knows the driver und the horse."

Shortly after three o'clock that afternoon Miss Bailey and Doctor Ingraham were standing beside a little bed in Gouverneur Hospital.

"Nathan is a horrible little liar," said the doctor genially. "Morris will be as well as ever in a week or so. The horse stood on his foot and bruised it rather badly, but he has all his fingers and his ring too. Haven't you, old man?"

"Yiss ma'an, yiss sir; I got it here," answered the boy, as, with his uninjured hand, he drew up his battered trophy, hung about his neck on a piece of antiseptic gauze. "It's from sure gold und you gives it to me over that cat. But say, Teacher, Missis Bailey, horses ain't like cats."

"No, dear, I know; that was a wicked horse."

"Yiss ma'an; I guess you don't know 'bout horses. You said boys should make all times what is loving mit horses, but horses don't make what is lovin' mit boys. Und my mamma she says it's a foolishness you should make what is lovin' mit somebody sooner somebody don't make what is loving mit you."

"That," said Dr. Ingraham, with a reproachful eye upon Miss Bailey, "is one of the truest truths in all the laws and the prophets. 'A foolishness' it certainly is."

"That's how my mamma says," Morris plaintively continued. "Und I guess she knows. I done it und now I'm got a sickness over it."

"Of course you have," acquiesced the doctor. "So have I. We all get it at times and its name is - "

"Don't listen to him, honey," Miss Bailey interrupted.

"You will be all right again in a few weeks."

"Years," interposed the doctor.

"And while you are here I shall come to see you every day to bring you books and candy and to tell you stories."

"Tell me one now," Morris implored. "Take off your hat so I can put mine head at your necktie, und then you should tell me that story over, 'Once upon some time when that world was young.'"

It was nearly five o'clock when Miss Bailey gently disengaged herself and set out upon her uptown way. She passed from the hush of the hospital walls and halls into another phase of her accountability. Upon the steps, a woman, wild-eyed and dishevelled, was hurling an unintelligible mixture of pleading and abuse upon the stalwart frame of Patrick Brennan's father, the policeman on the beat. The woman tore her hair, wept, and beat her breast, but Mr. Brennan's calm was impassive.

"You can't see him," he remarked. "Didn't they tell you that Thursday was visiting day? Well, and isn't this Choos-day? Go home now and shut up."

"Mine Gott, he will die!" wailed the woman.

"Not he," said Mr. Brennan. "Go home now and come back on Thursday. There's no good standing there. And there's no good in coming back in half an hour. You'll not see him before Thurs-day."

The woman fell to wild weeping and her sympathetic

neighbours followed suit.

"Ach, mine little boy!" she wailed. "Mine arme little Morris!" And "arme little Morris" the neighbours echoed.

"Morris Mogilewsky?" asked Miss Bailey.

"Yes ma'an," answered Mr. Brennan with a shrug.

"Yes ma'an," cried the neighbours in shrill chorus.

"Yes ma'an," wailed the woman. "Mine Morris. They makes I shouldn't to see him. They takes him here the while he gets killed off of a horse."

"Killed und chawed off of a horse," shrieked the comforting neighbours.

"And are you his mother?" pursued Miss Bailey.

"Yes ma'an," they all answered as before.

"Very well, I think I can take you to see him. But not if you are going to be noisy."

A stillness as of death settled upon Mrs. Mogilewsky as she sank down at Miss Bailey's feet in dumb appeal. And Constance Bailey saw in the eyes, so like Morris's, fixed upon her face, a world of misery which she had surely though innocently wrought.

Dr. Ingraham was summoned and bent to Miss Bailey's will. A few moments later Morris's languid gaze embraced his mother, his teacher, and his doctor. The latter found Mrs. Mogilewsky's woe impervious to any soothing. "Chawed off of a horse!" she whimpered. "All the child what I got, chawed off of a horse!"

"Wicked old horse!" ejaculated Teacher.

"Crazy old Teacher!" snorted Mrs. Mogilewsky. "Fool old Teacher! I sends my little boy on the school so he should the English write und talk und the numbers learn so he comes - through the years maybe - American man, und she learns him foolishness over dogs und cats und horses. Crazy, crazy, crazy!"

"Oh, come now. That's rather strong," remonstrated Doctor Ingraham, with a quizzical glance at Miss Bailey. Mrs. Mogilewsky wheeled towards her benefactress.

"Do you know Morris's teacher?" she asked eagerly. "Ach, lady, kind lady, tell me where is her house; I like I shall tell her how she make sickness on my little boy. He lays on the bed over her. I like I should tell her somethings."

"Mrs. Mogilewsky," began Miss Bailey, gently, "there is nothing you could say to her that would make her more sorry than she is. She is broken-hearted already, and if you don't stop talking like that you will make her cry. And then Morris would surely cry too; shouldn't you, dearie?"

"Teacher, yiss ma'an," quavered Morris.

"You!" groaned Mrs. Mogilewsky. "Be you Morris's teacher? Gott, how I makes mistakes! So you learn him that foolishness extra so he gets chawed off of horses?"

"Nonsense," interposed the doctor. "Miss Bailey is ridiculously fond of that child of yours."

"So-o-oh," began Mrs. Mogilewsky. "So-o-oh, she ain't done it extra?"

"Purposely? Of course not," answered the doctor.

"Ach, well, I should better maybe, excuse her." Mrs. Mogilewsky, placated and bland, resumed: "I excuse her the while she ain't so awful old. She makes, sometimes, mistakes too. I like you should come - the both - on my house for see me some day. That makes me glad in mine heart."

"Oh mamma, mamma," cried Morris, "they couldn't to come by our house. They is Krishts. She is Krishts und he is Krishts. From long she tells me. Und you says, you says - "

"Think shame," his mother admonished him. "Ain't you seen how she is lovin' mit you? Und Morris, mine golden one, I am all times lovin' mit somebody what is lovin' mit you. Ain't I excused her over it und made her invitation on my house?

"And we shall be delighted," said the doctor, as he led the speechless Miss Bailey away. "It is uncommonly good of you to have forgiven her. But, as you, with keenest insight, discern, she is not very old. Perhaps she will reform."

"Reform! I hate the very word," sighed Miss Bailey, for the day had been trying and her discouragement was great. "I've been trying to reform these people ever since I came down here. I've failed and failed and failed; misunderstood time and time again; made mistake after mistake. And now I've nearly killed that boy. The woman was right. It was all my fault."

"It might be better - " began the Doctor and halted. "You might be happier if you - "

"Resigned?" suggested Teacher. "Yes, sometimes I think I shall." "Do," said Doctor Ingraham. "That's a capital beginning."

www.ingramcontent.com/pod-product-compliance
Lightning Source LLC
Chambersburg PA
CBHW031349170626
46807CB00002B/886